Library of Congress
Registration Number TXu 2-412-440 Date January 21, 2024

Cover Design: Susan E. Lewis
Company Logo Design: Susan E. Lewis
  • americasfairydogmother.com
  • selsignaturecollection.com
  • puppyparentbootcamp.com
Page Layout and Template Design: Susan E. Lewis

Printed and bound in the United States of America
ISBN Number: 9798992134988

Contents

Susan E. Lewis
AKC Canine Good Citizen Evaluator and Celebrity Puppy Trainer

Dear Puppy Parents,

I am thrilled to introduce the *Puppy Parents Playbook and the "10 Good Puppy Steps"*, a valuable resource that will guide you and your fellow Puppy Parents toward becoming responsible, loving, and well-prepared caregivers. This resource will enhance your puppy's quality of life and contribute to the well-being of countless shelter dogs in need of loving adoption homes.

HOPE: Help One Puppy Every Day!

The animal services system is in dire need of change. Approximately 6.5 million companion animals enter U.S. shelters every year. The "10 Good Puppy Steps" education program empowers you to help prevent 3.1 million dogs from entering animal shelters, and it could save the lives of 390,000 of the 920,000 shelter animals deliberately euthanized annually in the United States (ASPCA).

The *Puppy Parents Playbook* offers the ideal solution to assist overwhelmed parents who are lost between Dream Dog Street and Puppy Reality Blvd. This tool will help you confidently navigate your first year of Puppy Parenthood. I highly recommend purchasing the award-winning online class at *puppyparentbootcamp.com* and the *Puppy Parents Playbook*. Before welcoming a new puppy into your family, get a pre-Puppy Parent education at puppyparentbootcamp.com. Responsible dog ownership involves proper training, socialization, healthcare, and love. These essential steps ensure a harmonious relationship with your puppy and set a commendable example for your children and others.

Sincerely,

Susan E. Lewis
America's Fairy Dogmother

Contact:
puppyparentbootcamp.com
americasfairydogmother.com
selsignaturecollection.com

Good Puppy Step 1

Talk to an American Kennel Club

dog trainer and veterinarian before

acquiring a Puppy!

What About Us?

The disagreeable blinking cursor and I had a long-standing irritation. We never liked each other much and needed space! The enticing sound of the waves splashed against the yacht's hull; delightful aromas drifted from the chef's kitchen into my cabin. The December noonday sun smiled over the ancient city of Genoa, Italy, inviting me to explore its labyrinthine streets. My wardrobe screamed Boston proper. However, I chose not to freeze over familiar formality to walk through the city. Classic dressage boots, riding breeches, and my favorite sweatshirt worked. I left the 5-star crew precisely performing their duties and writer's block behind. The cobblestone pathways meandered like a timeline of history since the 4th or 5th millennium BC, worn smooth by the footsteps of past generations. The scent of the sea wafted on a gentle breeze mingling with the music of talented street performers, lured me deeper into the dog-friendly city's heart.

Small family shops and friendly people are the heartbeat of this enchanting Italian city. Whether exploring a centuries-old market, stepping into a cozy café or a family-run trattoria, you'll find that the people of Genoa are eager to share their culture, cuisine, and stories with visitors. Their genuine hospitality and a deep sense of community give the city a unique and welcoming atmosphere. From sipping an espresso at a corner café to selecting fresh produce at the local market, you'll experience the heart and soul of Genoa in these interactions.

Palaces line the streets, true architectural marvels that whispered tales of wealth and opulence from centuries ago. I couldn't help but pause and marvel at each one, imagining the pampered puppies and people who once lived within those storied walls. Their facades were adorned with ornate details, intricate wrought-iron balconies, and weathered frescoes that held secrets lost to time.

Feeling liberated from the blank page and bleeping blinking cursor, I wandered with no particular destination until I felt called to follow a series of winding alleys, taking spontaneous turns. One such turn led me to a place of profound serenity and spirituality, a hidden gem that defied the bustling city outside. The aged, wooden door of the church creaked open, welcoming me into a hushed world of history, mystery, and centuries of secrets. As I stepped inside, the dimly lit interior revealed itself gradually as my eyes adjusted to the muted light. And there, before me, was the heart of this ancient sanctuary of a breathtaking 800-year-old church.

I was entranced by the sunlight filtered through the vibrant, centuries-old stained-glass windows casting an ethereal, kaleidoscopic dance of colors upon the stone floor. Memories of my childhood resurfaced as I recalled my beautiful mother showing me stained-glass windows for the first time. Those cherished memories filled me with wonder and awe. A familiar, intense sound woke me out of contemplation. "Woof! Woof!"

The sincere gaze of the canine church visitor, those two blue pools of sorrow, held an undeniable depth of emotion. It was as if this four-legged messenger had channeled a universal question, asking, **"What about us"**? As I locked eyes with the dog, and in that moment, a profound understanding flowed between us.

With a heart full of empathy, I listened as the dog continued to communicate with a series of urgent "Woof! Woof!" It was clear that the upset canine was seeking an answer to a question that had long troubled many who shared its sentiment. The chills of truth surged through my body, and I felt a deep sense of responsibility to address this unspoken concern. The dog's question was simple yet profound: "Why is the sound of silent sermons about responsible stewardship of animals and the planet deafening in the church?"

In that sacred space, as I beheld the image of Jesus lying in a manger, surrounded by the animals he loved, the answer seemed self-evident. The teachings of compassion, love, and responsible stewardship that Jesus embodied should extend to God's creation, the Earth's creatures, and the planet we call home.

I sat down in the pew, overwhelmed by the clarity of the dog's message. The upset dog had become a messenger, a voice for the voiceless, asking us to reevaluate our priorities and acknowledge our moral responsibility toward the environment and its inhabitants.

With a deep sense of purpose, I realized that the question posed by the dog was not only for me but for all who heard its message. It was a call to action, a reminder that the church's teachings should encompass the spiritual and physical world, the creatures that share our planet, and the urgent need for responsible stewardship. God spoke to me through a dog! I resolved to create and share the **"10 Good Puppy Steps"** Pre-Puppy Parent program with the world.

As I left the church, the question continued to echo in my heart and mind, a catalyst for change and a reminder that we are all connected in our responsibility to care for the Earth and its creatures. The Dog's simple yet profound query opened the door to a deeper understanding of the church's role in advocating for the welfare of all living beings and the planet during the 6th mass extinction authored by human beings. Our attention to the pressing climate change issues and the ongoing biodiversity crisis emphasizes the importance of collective action and change at this critical juncture in history.

The warmth of the city's bells of freedom rang in the church tower on that brisk, starry Christmas Eve and welcomed the faithful. My eyes welled up with tears listening to the sweet music of the people singing "Silent Night" in Italian, filling the candlelit ancient church. I realized "Silent Night" was first performed on Christmas Eve 1818 at St Nikolaus parish church in Oberndorf bei Salzburg, Austria, approximately 6 hours north of Genoa. When the song's composers, Joseph Mohr, and Franz Xaver Gruber, created this iconic carol, they blessed the world with a gift that has since become a symbol of peace and the Christmas season transcending cultural and linguistic boundaries.

I strained my ears, hoping to hear the familiar, longing bark of my Golden companion, but the silence was still deafening. **What about us?** I thought as I scanned the church for my disheartened friend, yearning to impart a message of hope. Just like my faithful companion, I realized I needed to become a messenger, a voice for the voiceless.

What about dogs, who teach us to allow our hearts to take flight and remember that we are all made from God's breath of light? Our creator, human, and animal, endowed us with the ability to be sentient beings, acknowledging that all creation deserves a life free from unnecessary suffering. These natural, inalienable rights are absolute and cannot be taken away, transferred to another person, or nullified by law, custom, or belief.

In September 2023, Ojai, California, marked a historic moment by becoming the first city in America to recognize the legal rights of nonhuman animals, trailing behind several countries that have officially recognized animals as sentient beings, working towards a more just and compassionate world.

Summary

"What About Us?" unfolds amidst the beautiful setting of Genoa, Italy, as Susan, feeling trapped by writer's block aboard a yacht, decides to explore the city. The vibrant streets and welcoming locals captivate the protagonist, revealing the heart and soul of Genoa through its culture, cuisine, and warmth.

While wandering the historic streets, Susan stumbles upon an ancient church, where a profound encounter with a dog, the unspoken messenger, communicates a heartfelt plea through urgent barks, questioning the absence of discussions on responsible stewardship for animals and the planet within the church.

This poignant moment triggers a revelation within Susan, prompting a reevaluation of priorities and a recognition of the interconnectedness of all beings. The message conveyed by the dog becomes a catalyst for a deeper understanding of the church's role in advocating for the welfare of all living beings and the planet, emphasizing the need for responsible stewardship and compassion.

Feeling moved and inspired; Susan Lewis resolves to become a messenger echoing the dog's call for a more compassionate world. This leads to the commitment to create and share the **"10 Good Puppy Steps"** pre-Puppy Parent program, aiming to raise awareness and promote responsible stewardship for the planet and its inhabitants.

The story concludes by reflecting on the significance of collective action and change in addressing pressing issues like climate change and biodiversity crises. It references real-world events, such as Ojai, California, recognizing the legal rights of nonhuman animals, highlighting ongoing efforts towards a more just and compassionate world for all beings.

Good Puppy Step 2

Create a Monthly Puppy Budget

- Studies show the average lifetime cost of caring for all-size dog breeds is $50,000.

- Puppy 0 - 12 months: The estimated cost is between $3,333 - $10,000.

Wings of Unity

On February 7th, 1632, Governor Winthrop and his party discovered a hidden treasure in a charming New England town; there lay a serene and picturesque spot known as Spot Pond. The life-giving waters lie in the heart of Middlesex Fells Reservation State Park, Stoneham, MA. It is an oasis of calm amidst the world's chaos, where the whispers of nature meet the thunder of life's mysteries. On a brisk fall day, the Wings of Unity retook flight.

Every morning, the star-spangled sky gracefully yielded to the radiant sunrise. The assembly of diverse wildlife, drawn by the communal harmony of the Canada geese, eagerly awaited their daily performance. The geese's feathers, adorned in black, white, and gray, symbolized unity as they took to the skies with unwavering determination. Their synchronized flight at sunrise resembled a tribute to the flag-raising ritual, a display of unwavering allegiance to the American spirit.

A whispering rumble of thunder took flight above Spot Pond. With a unified grace, they took to the crisp autumn sky, flying in a V-shaped formation that stood for victory! The whispering thunder gradually became a honking symphony as they flew over my parents' house at precisely 6 a.m. I rushed to the window to witness the spectacle, and amidst the flock, I recognized the stout figure of a familiar farm goose adopted by the flock, Uncle Tucker. Uncle Tucker had sheltered the goslings under his protective wings during nap times in the summer, earning the gratitude of their parents.

The flock looked like a moving sculpture against the canvas of the changing leaves and morning sun. The trees celebrated the Canada geese flight of freedom from near extinction in the 1950s by shedding golden and flaming red fall leaves like confetti. These geese were not ordinary birds; they are respected and protected guardians of Spot Pond, its timeless keepers. They held within them the wisdom of countless seasons, passed down from generation to generation. They knew when it was time to migrate when the whispers of the wind told tales of distant lands and new horizons.

Sage, the lead goose, a wise elder with a steely gaze, guided the way. In their formation, each bird contributed to the greater good, their wings creating an aerodynamic masterpiece that allowed them to glide through the heavens with unparalleled efficiency. The flock encouraged the young goslings and reminded them of their lessons about the importance of staying together as a united flock.

Mother Mariah, one of the elder geese, diligently taught the goslings the importance of the V-formation, explaining how it reduced wind resistance, facilitated efficient communication, and conserved energy for the long journey ahead. Canada geese could cover a thousand miles a day in favorable weather conditions. The elder geese also instilled the values of loyalty and teamwork, demonstrating how to protect a wounded member of the flock by carrying them through the skies, showcasing the essence of unity and strength within the Wings of Unity.

They taught the young birds how to protect a wounded flock member and carry them through the skies, demonstrating the bonds that bound the flock together. They taught the goslings that they were not just individuals but part of their flock, the Wings of Unity, each with a role to play.

In the same way that the lessons of the Canadian geese emphasize unity, cooperation, and mutual support, it is time for the United States to join the global community of nations that have officially recognized animals as sentient beings. Canada geese serve as a powerful symbol of these principles, where each flock member plays a crucial role for the greater good, and their synchronized flight exemplifies the strength of unity.

Similarly, recognizing animals as sentient beings is a step towards building a compassionate world. It acknowledges the interconnectedness of all living beings and the importance of extending compassion and ethical treatment to animals. The lessons of the Canada geese underscore the values of loyalty and teamwork, demonstrating how they protect wounded members of their flock by carrying them through the skies. This essence of unity and strength should extend to our treatment of animals.

By officially recognizing animals as sentient beings, the United States can affirm the importance of their well-being and welfare. It signifies a commitment to acknowledge the intrinsic value of animals, ensuring that they are not treated merely as commodities but as beings capable of intelligent thought, communication, feeling pain, joy, and a range of emotions.

Just as the Canada geese's synchronized flight at sunrise symbolizes an unwavering allegiance to the American spirit, recognizing animals as sentient beings aligns with the nation's justice, empathy, and compassion values. This shows a dedication to promoting a culture where animals are given honor and consideration, and their protection and well-being are ensured.

The global movement towards recognizing animals as sentient beings is a significant step in the evolution of our understanding of the ethical treatment of animals. It reflects the principles of unity and collective responsibility that the Canada geese demonstrate daily. We observe geese flying together as a cohesive flock and learn the value of unity and cooperation. Similarly, recognizing the sentience of animals reminds us of our collective duty to build a more empathetic world that values all living beings. It is time for the United States to become part of this international flock, working towards a world where animals are valued as sentient beings, and their well-being is a shared priority.

Pet Parent Paradox

In 2022, Americans spent a staggering $136.8 billion on their beloved pets. It prompts us to ponder a critical question: What holds a higher cost: the love and care we lavish upon our animal companions or the paradoxical tragedy that befalls nearly a million innocent shelter animals who pay the ultimate price of life each year?

This financial comparison transcends numerical figures; it delves into the core of our societal values and ethical priorities. Drawing inspiration from the harmonious flight of Canada geese, we, too, can unify and confront the challenges besieging our broken animal shelter system.

The solution lies within our collective commitment to fostering awareness, providing necessary resources, and advocating for change. It is paramount to understand that these challenges, although daunting, are surmountable. We possess the power to create a more compassionate and humane framework for caring for needy animals.

- Joining the global movement to recognize animals as sentient beings echoes the unity and allegiance symbolized by Canadian geese's synchronized flight at sunrise. This recognition aligns with our nation's values of justice, empathy, and compassion. It signifies our commitment to creating a society. Their rights and welfare should be safeguarded.

- The "**No Breeding Years**" proposal offers a compassionate solution to tackle shelter overpopulation. This initiative necessitates a temporary halt in all non-essential breeding, a measure that can drastically reduce the number of animals entering shelters. Through this mandatory breeding hiatus, we have the power to save countless lives and increase the chances of animal adoptions.

- Furthermore, promoting responsible pet ownership remains a pivotal component of our approach. The "**10 Good Puppy Steps**" program guides individuals through their first year of Puppy Parenthood, educating them on proper pet care, training, and the enduring commitment required to provide a loving and stable home for animals.

Summary

The "Wings of Unity" begins in a serene New England town where Spot Pond, nestled in Middlesex Fells Reservation State Park, serves as a sanctuary amid life's tumult. The story unfolds with majestic Canada geese, a symbol of unity, soaring across the sky each morning in a mesmerizing display of synchronized flight.

Their V-shaped formation signifies victory, unity, and allegiance to the American spirit. Among them is Uncle Tucker, a farm goose revered for protecting goslings in summer. The geese, timeless keepers of Spot Pond, embody wisdom passed through generations, teaching young goslings the essence of unity, teamwork, and loyalty.

Their flight holds a profound message for humanity—recognizing animals as sentient beings. This echoes their cooperative nature and promotes compassion and ethical treatment towards animals. Aligning with American values of justice and empathy, this recognition emphasizes honoring animals' intrinsic value, ensuring their welfare, and fostering a compassionate society.

Reflecting on staggering pet care expenses juxtaposed with the plight of shelter animals underscores societal values. Inspired by the geese's harmony, addressing challenges in the animal shelter system becomes a collective responsibility, achievable through awareness, resources, and advocating for change.

Proposals like the **"No Breeding Year"** aim to curtail shelter overpopulation by temporarily halting non-essential breeding, while responsible pet ownership initiatives like the "10 Good Puppy Steps" educate individuals on proper pet care and commitment.

In a narrative interwoven with the geese's lessons, "Wings of Unity" urges the United States to join the global movement recognizing animals as sentient beings. It signifies a commitment to creating a compassionate world, drawing parallels between the geese's unity and the need for collective action to safeguard animal rights and welfare.

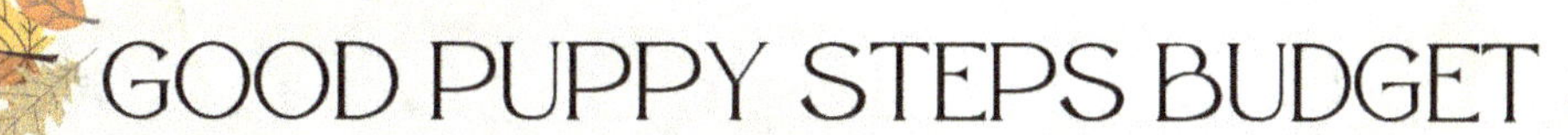 GOOD PUPPY STEPS BUDGET 

DATE	TOTAL INCOME	TOTAL SAVINGS	EMERGENCY FUND
CATEGORY	ESTIMATED EXPENSE	ACTUAL EXPENSE	DIFFERENCE
FOOD			
MEDICAL EXPENSES			
PUPPY PARENT BOOTCAMP			
DOG TRAINING			
CHEWS & TREAT TOYS & PUZZLES			
LEASH & HARNESS COLLAR/CRATE/BED			
PET INSURANCE GPS ID/CHIP/TAG			
GROOMING			
DAY CARE & BOARDING			
LEGAL FEES REGISTRATION			

 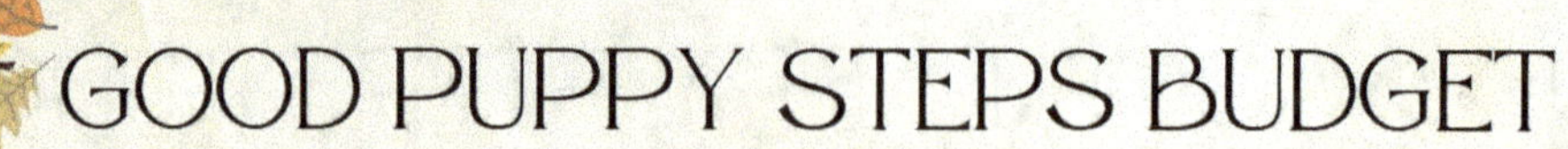 # GOOD PUPPY STEPS BUDGET 

YEAR	TOTAL INCOME	TOTAL SAVINGS	EMERGENCY FUND
NAME	ACTUAL EXPENSE	MONTH TOTAL	YEAR TOTAL
JANUARY			
FEBRUARY			
MARCH			
APRIL			
MAY			
JUNE			
JULY			
AUGUST			
SEPTEMBER			
OCTOBER			
NOVEMBER			
DECEMBER			

Good Puppy Step 3

Get Experience Working with Dogs

whether you have previously owned a dog or are thinking

about becoming a Puppy Parent for the first time.

Pinecrest Abbey and Aria's Bells of Freedom

In a charming winter country setting, nestled in the heart of the serene setting of Pinecrest Abbey, Aria, the Golden Retriever, whose wisdom was a beacon of enlightenment and grace as enchanting as the snow-covered landscape around her. Aria's name was a melodic ode to the spirit of a Christmas carol that echoed through the frosty air, weaving an intricate tapestry of harmony and warmth.

My life is far removed from the bustling city lights; it is an idyllic existence. My days are spent amidst 1000 acres of rolling hills and crisp New England mornings, except for today. I felt concerned. The whisper of the wind through the frosted trees carried the smell of disturbing news about my canine friends. I resolved not to get my frozen fiery fur in a fury over it. I am attuned to the rhythms of the seasons, and my life is guided by the voice of God, a presence that I had come to understand as the benevolent orchestrator of my path.

It was upon one such winter's Christmas Eve, as the silver moon cast its ethereal glow upon the pristine snow, that I felt an unshakeable calling within my heart. I had observed the ignorance that seemed to cloud the minds of my human companions on too many occasions. It was a veil that obscured their understanding of the bonds shared with my loyal canine friends, General, Trooper, and Koda, much like the fog that veiled the landscape on a frosty morning. I am a frosty force of nature. My momma raised no fool! Sometimes, humans are such "treasures" that I want to bury them permanently!

I need to impart a lesson and unveil their ignorance's depths. It was a form of blindness, a spell cast by the author of lies that concealed the value of love within my furry brethren. Much like the stories of old, their hearts need to be awakened on this holy night.

I sat by the candlelit frozen window, my gentle amber eyes glistening as I gazed upon the stars that adorned the winter sky. I prayed to God, seeking divine intervention, to speak to my human companions' hearts and guide them toward enlightenment. My prayer was filled with a deep yearning, a fervent hope that the ignorance would be dispelled and the love they shared would flourish.

God, in all His wisdom, chose to answer my prayer on this sacred Christmas Eve, weaving the fabric of destiny in a powerful and transformative manner. He knew that the lessons of the heart were most impactful when learned through experience. Thus, the dreams were cast.

The whistling wind billowed a powerful snow drift. The first dream was cast. A man named William Kingston, a devoted forester dreamed that he was transformed into his beloved 8-year-old German Shepherd, General. As General, he witnessed the beauty of the forest he had planted, felt the joy of locating lost souls within its embrace, and, most profoundly, he experienced the betrayal of being surrendered to shelter. The pain of abandonment that William had unwittingly inflicted upon General was etched into his soul, a lesson learned through the eyes of a loyal friend.

After waking from this powerful dream, William no longer bore the weight of his past mistakes. He rushed to the shelter, where he reunited with General. Together, they planted trees and located people lost in the forest. William founded the **"General Foundation,"** a non-profit organization dedicated to helping retired Police Service Dogs like General find loving homes, honoring the faithful companion who had changed his life.

Rooftop icicles dropped, and the second dream was cast. A woman named Emily Ashford dreamt she turned her into Trooper, a playful and loving Springer Spaniel who had been relegated to the garage for 14 years. Emily felt the isolation and pain that Trooper had endured. She observed herself callously disregarding Trooper's cries for help and replaced him with a puppy. The dream was an awakening, a harsh mirror reflecting on her callousness that cut through her heart.

Awakening from her dream, Emily rushed to Trooper's side, showering him with love and affection. She decided to make amends for her past behavior by creating the **"Trooper Foundation,"** a non-profit organization dedicated to helping older dogs find new, loving homes. She understood the worth of the bond they shared, and she was determined to ensure other dogs like Trooper found the love and care they deserved.

The bells rang in the church tower, signaling the commencement of midnight mass. I heard the people sing my favorite song, "The Bells of Freedom." I knew the third most powerful dream of all was cast. A young woman named Lily Winthrop dreamed she became Koda, the Husky puppy she had been given as a gift, without understanding the consequences. Koda's traumatic journey revealed the depth of abandonment and helplessness that Lily's actions had caused. The dream served as a powerful reminder that animals are not gifts!

Awakening with tears in her eyes, Lily realized her mistake and took swift action to make amends. She started a campaign called **"Koda's Law,"** which advocated for legislation making it illegal to give an animal as a gift, ensuring that no more pets would face the same heartbreak that Koda had experienced.

With the lessons learned from these dreams, the lives of my friends General, Trooper, and Koda improved immeasurably. Their owners, inspired by the transformations they had undergone, dedicated themselves to giving back and ensuring that no other pets would suffer due to ignorance or neglect.

In this enchanting winter country New England setting, the warmth of love, compassion, and enlightenment prevailed. Aria, with her unwavering devotion to the lessons of love, watched as her prayers were answered and the bonds between humans and their canine companions were rekindled with newfound understanding and tenderness. The magic of Christmas had touched their hearts, and it would continue to warm them through the seasons, ensuring that the love they shared would flourish and endure.

Summary

"Pinecrest Abbey and Aria's Bells of Freedom" unfolds in the tranquil setting of Pinecrest Abbey, where Aria, a Golden Retriever, resides amidst the wintry beauty. Embodying the spirit of a Christmas carol, Aria feels compelled to address the ignorance that obscures the bond between humans and their canine companions.

Aria prays for divine guidance to enlighten her human companions. Through dreams orchestrated by God, three individuals experience transformative journeys as their perspectives shift by stepping into the paws of their loyal canine friends on a sacred Christmas Eve.

William Kingston dreams of becoming his German Shepherd, General, and experiencing the joy of the forest and the pain of abandonment. Inspired, William reunites with General and establishes a foundation to aid retired Police Service Dogs, honoring his faithful companion.

Emily Ashford's dream as Trooper, a neglected Springer Spaniel, leads her to acknowledge her neglect and create the Trooper Foundation, which is dedicated to rehoming older dogs.

Lily Winthrop, dreaming as Koda, her Husky puppy, faces the cold sting of abandonment, a trauma so profound that it shatters her heart, leading Lily to initiate "Koda's Law," advocating against giving animals as gifts.

These dreams foster profound changes; General, Trooper, and Koda find better lives, while their owners, inspired by the dreams, dedicate themselves to aiding neglected animals. Love, compassion, and understanding triumph, ensuring the enduring bond between humans and their beloved animal companions in the enchanting setting of Pinecrest Abbey.

Good Puppy Step 4

Learn How to Speak Dog

Dog communication refers to the exchange of information between dogs and also between dogs and humans. You and your dog can communicate through various behaviors and actions such as body, scent, verbal and non-verbal language.

I discovered that my dressage horse, Sambuca, did not like men when he tossed my father off! My dear father sat bewildered on the beautifully manicured front lawn of our charming New England home. Sambuca's fear was palpable, a painful memory of a man who had mistreated him. The power of patience and love shared a strong bond, leading to mutual healing. Slowly but surely, these elements melted away the terrible memories that had prevented Sambuca from thoroughly enjoying the gift of life.

Every day after the high school bus dropped me off, I was at Meadowbrook Farm. This farm, which had operated as a dairy farm since 1928, had transitioned into a supplier of landscape materials, many of which were provided by the horses boarding there. I had learned to be fastidious at Canterwood Lake Grove, where I had spent weeks, and this quality extended to the two or three hours I spent on stall cleaning, feeding, grooming, and dressage lessons. Some days, I would brush, talk, and sing to my spirited and brave chestnut Morab. His countenance transformed from timidity to tenacity. His forehead was decorated with a white diamond between his intelligent brown eyes. With proper care, he transfigured into a stunning steed. Little by little, Sambuca began to trust me. It took a year before he allowed me to brush his face gently. Together, we overcame life's challenges, relying on each other for support.

Sambuca waited patiently on the crossties as I finished cleaning the stall. Soon, I expected my mother to arrive and take me home. She made the Thanksgiving pies and prepared for dinner at my grandmother's house. The brisk fall whistling winds blew outside. My barn friends had already gone home. The November chill in the air suggested I put a winter blanket on Sambuca.

I took Sambuca off the crossties, walked him into his stall, and closed the bottom Dutch door. I remained inside the stall with Sambuca. Unexpectedly, old Mr. Meadows saw me sporting overalls and waddled into the barn. My polite but frigid greeting expressed my discomfort toward the stranger. I remembered Mom's manners matter lessons. Mr. Meadow's jubilant greeting was too familiar, as we had not been adequately introduced. He ignored my nervous disdain. I was expected to behave in ways that did not include greeting strange men alone in a barn. Sambuca immediately felt my discomfort. My 1500-pound protector placed himself between me and the Dutch door until Mr. Meadows left the barn. No words are required!

Relieved to hear my mother arrive, I quickly draped Sambuca's winter blanket and fastened the straps. We said goodnight until tomorrow. I remained silent on the way home. I resolved to help my mother with Thanksgiving preparations. My Boston proper mother was bookish, impeccably dressed in the finest clothes, and poised. She was as sweet as the pies she made and never cursed. Except when a nor'easter named Mom exploded when she accidentally dropped a pie on the kitchen floor! A symphony of words spontaneously combusted from her tiny frame, accompanied by classical music, filled our house.

My Grandmother's colonial house on Crown Court was built in 1926. Thanksgiving commenced. The familiar whimsical Hummels sat above the front door; an antique 1940s phone rested on the kitchen table. I remember her kitchen was filled with delicious aromas. She played Christmas carols on the organ in the living room as our family gathered. The artificial tree decorated with vintage ornaments and lights sparkled. The blaze of the fireplace lit the room and highlighted a particular curiosity hanging from the mahogany mantle. It was a string of antique etched brass bells. The larger jingle bells emitted a low tone. The tiny bells rang out in a high pitch. My musical Grandmother kindly gave the bells to me.

Summary

"No Words Required" is a tale of profound connections centered around Susan's bond with Sambuca, her dressage horse with a troubled past. The story unfolds against the backdrop of a New England home and Meadowbrook Farm, where Susan diligently tends to Sambuca, through patience and care. The narrative weaves together trust-building moments, overcoming past traumas, and the silent thought communication between the protagonist and the horse.

A pivotal event occurs when Susan and Sambuca face an unexpected visitor at the farm. This reveals the depth of their connection as Sambuca instinctively shields Susan from discomfort. Against this backdrop, the story delves into familial traditions, Thanksgiving preparations, and the warmth of gatherings at Grandmother's colonial house.

Through vivid imagery and nuanced descriptions, the narrative paints a picture of resilience, the power of understanding without words, and the enduring bonds between humans and animals, culminating in a heartfelt tale of mutual trust, healing, and the unspoken language of companionship.

Good Puppy Step 5

Learn How to Understand Dog Behavior

Through centuries of coexistence, the behavior of dogs has been significantly shaped by their interaction with humans, resulting in their remarkable ability to understand and engage with us in highly intelligent ways.

Paws of Redemption:
Princess Missy's Story

Princess Missy stood on the brink of existence, her destiny hanging in the balance within a brief 24-hour timeframe, during which we became each other's saviors in the face of life's uncertainties. She was a robust and amiable German Shepherd-Collie, yet she had weathered a regrettable succession of unexpected and severe tribulations. Evidently, the clamorous and congested shelter surroundings had exacted a heavy emotional toll on her. It was unmistakable that what she yearned for most was a caring and nurturing home.

In the subsequent week, Princess Missy underwent a process of emotional recovery. Initially, she spent the better part of two days in deep slumber, punctuating her rest for the essential needs of nature and sustenance. As her physical and mental state gradually improved, a subtle change became evident: her previously tucked tail now stood raised, reflecting a shift in her disposition. However, it had its challenges. Addressing her tendencies to guard her food and toys required patience and understanding. The icy, distant gaze in her eyes and the low, ominous growl that emanated from her were stark manifestations of fear borne out of a series of unfortunate experiences wrought by human actions.

Coexisting with humans has a profound positive or negative influence on a dog's behavior. My dog's positive interactions with me played an essential role in shaping her confidence and respect. Dogs are highly social animals, and their interactions with humans significantly influence their behavior, emotional well-being, and ability to navigate the world around them, especially the new toy aisle at the store! Missy shopped for her toys and brought her treasures to the cash register herself.

I dedicated substantial effort towards establishing the fundamental underpinnings of trust between Princess Missy and me. Over time, this diligent endeavor yielded a robust and enduring connection characterized by mutual respect, kindness, love, and unwavering care. We reached an advanced level of intuitive synchronization through training exercises, allowing us to move as a unified entity, fostering a profound sense of harmony and togetherness.

One evening, Princess Missy voluntarily retreated to the farthest reaches of the house while I continued doing my homework into the late hours. An hour later, I decided to test the depth of our communication telepathically. I silently projected the command, "Princess Missy, Come Front!" Surprisingly, she promptly appeared by my side, her tail wagging enthusiastically. The sheer swiftness and accuracy of her response left me stunned.

One beautiful spring day, bathed in warm sunlight, we decided to stroll across a vast, lush field. As we walked, Princess Missy's ears laid flat against her head. She abruptly halted and fixed her gaze on something in the distance. Without delay, we froze, just inches away from a perilous and potentially deadly danger concealed within the grass. Regrettably, it was not a charming rabbit or an amicable squirrel that had garnered her attention. Fate had presented us with the presence of a venomous rattlesnake.

With utmost discretion and respect for the snake's formidable nature, we retraced our steps and cautiously selected an alternative path, wisely avoiding confrontation with this formidable reptile. Missy courageously had saved both our lives.

I soon discovered that Missy's capacity for deep empathy surpassed her courage. She consistently accompanied me on car rides, with one notable exception. On this particular occasion, I left my faithful canine companion home as I embarked on a scenic journey through a lush, picturesque valley. My destination was a nearby stable, where I planned to watch a friend's dressage riding lesson.

Two hours later, I commenced my return home with a deliberate and cautious approach, mindful not to disturb the horses peacefully grazing in the pastures along the tranquil country road. The sight before me was nothing short of enchanting: magnificent homes, sprawling ranches, and breathtaking landscapes, all concealed from the relentless hustle of modern life. Here, time seemed to stand still, and hawks gracefully soared through the gentle whispers of the changing winds.

However, the idyllic serenity was abruptly shattered when my car lost control on a treacherous mix of gravel and sand, sending it into a wild spin. In an instant, my vehicle crashed through a pasture fence, and the windshield shattered, scattering glass around me in what felt like a surreal slow-motion sequence. In desperation, I uttered, "Jesus, take the wheel!" Surrendering to a profound sense of vulnerability, I felt a release as I entrusted my life to God, believing it might end.

The telephone pole into which my car had collided head-on had effectively totaled it. Astonishingly, the spinning shards of glass came to a halt and miraculously spared me from harm. Frozen with fear and still gripping the steering wheel, my heart began to race. I awakened to a stark realization: I had narrowly escaped a life-threatening encounter, a moment when it seemed the forces of adversity had sought to claim my life.

I felt an intense urgency, akin to a butterfly striving to break free from its chrysalis, as I yearned to escape the confinement of my car. As I pushed the door open and stepped out, another car halted nearby. In that fleeting moment, a man sitting in the passenger seat made an attempt to exit, but the driver forcefully yanked him back into the car, and they sped away swiftly. My adeptness in survival skills had conditioned me to remain stoic and unfazed by the reactions of onlookers. Personal experiences have taught me to anticipate assistance from emotionally resilient women rather than men when facing an emergency. With the timely involvement of a police officer and three close friends from the barn, the situation was efficiently resolved within an hour. At that point, my overwhelming desire was to return home to my loyal dog's companionship.

Nurse Princess Missy intuitively detected an issue, revealing a remarkable canine empathy that surpassed the emotional capacities of humans. Being in her company, engaging in activities like playing fetch and taking walks, proved therapeutic in clearing mental clutter and recovering from the aftermath of the car accident. The close brush with fatality sparked a renewed commitment to seek protection and connection, leading me to delve into studying the Armor of God as outlined in the Bible. I am profoundly thankful to God for preserving my life, and Princess Missy's comforting presence played a redemptive role in my healing process.

Missy required a 5 a.m. potty break. We walked our usual route and happened upon a field covered with dew and a misty blanket of fog. I mistakenly thought it was safe to let my dog off the leash. Missy paced back and forth, looking for the perfect spot. Suddenly, she saw two coyotes crossing the field.

Her body language communicated a very alert and angry message. In a flash, I saw her chasing the coyotes about 150 yards. I worried the coyotes would overcome Missy. I thought I would never see her again! I yelled out her emergency come-on-command call: "CHICKEN!" She emerged from the fog, running towards me immediately. Princess Missy was a brave force of nature to take note of.

Missy needed a 5 a.m. bathroom break, so we followed our usual path and stumbled upon a field covered in dew, blanketed with misty fog. Believing it was safe, I made the error of unleashing my dog. Missy wandered around, searching for the perfect spot, when suddenly, she spotted two coyotes crossing the field. Her body language conveyed intense alertness and anger. In an instant, I witnessed her sprinting after the coyotes, covering about 150 yards. Concern gripped me, fearing that the coyotes might overpower her, and I dreaded the thought of losing her forever.

In desperation, I shouted her emergency recall command, "CHICKEN!" Miraculously, she emerged from the fog and sprinted directly toward me. Princess Missy proved to be a courageous and remarkable force of nature that left a lasting impression. The arms of God's powerful protection and paws of redemption saved both Princess Missy and me from severe fatal enemy attacks from the unseen realm. Armor up every day!

Summary

"Paws of Redemption: Princess Missy's Story" chronicles the profound bond between a resilient German Shepherd-Collie named Princess Missy and her human companion. Plagued by past tribulations, Missy longed for a nurturing home and underwent emotional recovery under her owner's care.

Through dedicated efforts, trust between Missy and her owner flourished, fostering a profound connection. Their unspoken communication reached a surprising pinnacle when Missy responded instantly to a silent command. Together, they navigated life's uncertainties, including a perilous encounter with a rattlesnake, where Missy's vigilance saved them both.

Their bond deepened further when Missy displayed empathetic instincts, offering solace and support after a life-threatening car accident. Missy's presence became a source of healing and comfort, leading her owner on a spiritual path to seek protection through the study of the Armor of God.

In a moment of danger, Missy's bravery shone as she chased off coyotes, exhibiting remarkable courage and survival instincts. Her resilience and protection mirrored God's powerful safeguarding, leaving an indelible impression on her owner and reinforcing the belief in divine protection.

Through these shared experiences of bravery, empathy, and survival, "Paws of Redemption: Princess Missy's Story" celebrates the enduring bond between a loyal canine companion and a human, woven through moments of danger, healing, and spiritual awakening.

Good Puppy Step 6

Discover the History and Mystery of Dogs

Uncover the enigmatic past and profound abilities of dogs. Discover the historical evolution of dogs and the fascinating bond between canines and humans.

Wolf Women Whisper Wisdom

I strolled amidst a sacred place filled with towering cathedrals. Sunbeams played through the branches, and brisk winds sent sparkling snow across the tranquil lake. The familiar scent of pine brought back memories. Riding my horse Sambuca through the breathtaking New England wilderness, I discovered the secret language and life of trees. The profound knowledge made the experience of trotting through ancient forests magical! Standing in awe before a 2000-year-old tree, I felt a sudden need to be still and listen, letting go of my insignificant worldly worries. At that moment, the voice of truth spoke to me.

"Did you blanket the Earth with forests from a tiny seed in the ground? Do you give forests the ability to filter out pollutants from the air and release oxygen? Did you give trees the ability to communicate with other trees, sending nutrients and warning messages through chemical signals?" Under the shady Pines where wild things grow, a network of roots grows deep in the ground, connecting trees that make forests work. The voice of truth said, "Do you give the forests the ability to regulate the temperature?"

Even a tree stump is a nature book! They teach humans how to read rings. The width of the rings tells you which years had lots of rain or drought. The voice of truth spoke again. "Do you send the rain to encourage mighty trees to stretch out their branches and grow food?" Trees never stop giving. Will you be a giving tree?

Yet sadly, people cut down an estimated 15 billion trees per year all over the world. What if Americans agreed to spend the estimated 6.1 billion dollars on planting forests instead of buying a Christmas tree for 20 years to help restore Earth? The calculated result is $6.1 billion × 20 years = 122 billion trees would be planted!

Forestry reports say that the average cost of planting a tree is $1, so 6.1 billion dollars would plant about 6.1 billion trees in 1 year to help reverse climate change authored by humans. There are additional expenses apart from planting trees that come with reforestation. It is important to note there are other planning and work preparation costs involved in reforestation projects.

Under the crisp winter sky of Big Bear Alpine Zoo, my journey continued. I found myself rekindling a connection with nature. The White mountains framed the backdrop as I encountered a Gray she-wolf, a sanctuary resident, with a tale of rescue and redemption. Each creature in this sanctuary has a narrative, a journey that led them to their present abode.

This particular she-wolf maintained a cautious distance from the crowd's clamor, avoiding the intrusive gaze of visitors armed with cameras. Her scrutiny of the human spectacle hinted at a profound curiosity. Amidst the snow play of two magnificent male wolves, their antics reminiscent of frolicking puppies, a genuine smile crept onto my face.

Yet, as I observed the oblivious visitors, I could not help but feel a pang of disappointment in their lack of respectful behavior. The lesson of treating wildlife with consideration and reverence is crucial. It is often overlooked. This prompted me to ponder: who truly belongs within the enclosures, the wild inhabitants or the humans? Which among us is more civilized? The answer, clear to me, was that the real threat to the environment stemmed from human actions, not wildlife.

My upbringing near Spot Pond, MA, instilled in me the virtues of silence, stillness, and the art of communication with both wild and domesticated creatures. Frequent visits to the Stone Zoo provided solace, offering enlightening conversations with the dedicated staff committed to the proper care of the animals.

Admitting a certain unease in human company, I confessed to feeling more at ease among the Gray wolves. The sensation of being at home in their presence was undeniable. I looked away from the she-wolf, careful not to challenge her with a direct stare. Slowly, I knelt and embraced silence as the disruptive crowd meandered by. The she-wolf sensed my unique distinction compared to the visitors. She approached me, closing the gap between our worlds. I listened respectfully and understood her lesson. Wolves teach us to allow our hearts to take flight and remember we are all made from God's breath of light. In this encounter, the dichotomy between humans and wild creatures became stark, emphasizing the significance of approaching nature with humility and understanding.

In the beginning,
God spoke the name of the Wolf before Earth began.
So, the bond became one between Wolf and Man.
The history of Wolves and Dogs is thousands of years old.
There is much work to be done before winning gold.
Dogs came to serve.
They came to play and dance.
They came to help us embrace life's chance.
Dogs teach us to allow our hearts to take flight and remember that we are all
made from God's breath of light!

Authored by: Susan Elizabeth Lewis

In the ancient tapestry of North America's wilderness, the story of wolves unfolds across epochs, from prehistoric times to the present day. Two iconic figures emerge among the diverse canines that once roamed the continent: the Dire wolf and the Gray wolf.

Long before humans left their indelible mark, the Dire wolf reigned supreme. A formidable predator, larger and stockier than its modern counterpart, it navigated the Pleistocene landscapes, embodying an apex predator's spirit. Meanwhile, the Gray wolf, or Timber wolf (Canis lupus), ran alongside the Dire wolf, adapting to the changing climates and ecosystems.

As time wove its intricate patterns, humans and wolves embarked on an unforeseen journey of companionship. The symbiotic relationship between these two sentient beings began as mutual survival instincts drew them closer. With their keen senses and pack mentality, wolves aided humans in hunting and protection; while humans, with their evolving intelligence, provided wolves with a steady food source.

This reciprocity blossomed into a transformative bond, leading to the domestication of wolves into dogs. Over generations, the cooperative connection deepened, marking the genesis of countless dog breeds that would become loyal companions to humankind.

Yet, as civilizations grew, so did the complexities of this alliance. Wolves faced persecution and near extinction, particularly in the 1800s, as humans expanded their territories. The wolf's haunting howl echoed through the mountains, a poignant lament for a species on the brink. Amidst the shadows of adversity, a comeback story unfolded. Propelled by a newfound understanding of ecosystems, conservation efforts led to the Gray wolf's resurgence. The 25th anniversary of the Gray wolf's reintroduction into Yellowstone National Park in 2020 marked a pivotal moment in this tale of survival.

One remarkable character in this saga is Journey, a Gray wolf who traversed a thousand miles from Oregon to Northern California, capturing the collective imagination as a symbol of resilience. Journey's odyssey underscored the wolf's indomitable spirit and innate drive to reclaim lost territories.

Today, Yellowstone National Park stands as a testament to the triumph of conservation. The park's landscape echoes with the harmonious chorus of wolf packs, totaling at least 108 individuals across ten packs as of January 2023. The Gray wolf's howl, once silenced, now resonates through the valleys, reminding us of the intricate dance between humans and wolves—a dance that continues to unfold across the vast tapestry of time.

Between 15 to 40 thousand years ago, a pivotal divergence occurred as dogs forged a distinct path away from their ancestral wolves, embarking on a unique companionship with humans. The intricate tapestry of dog breeds began weaving in the last 1 to 2 thousand years, with the majority of breeds taking shape in the relatively recent span of 100 to 200 years.

The behavioral nuances of dogs have been profoundly shaped by their intricate interactions with humans. While wolves and dogs share a common ancestry, their paths have diverged, manifesting in notable differences. These distinctions encompass unique reproductive cycles, shifts in prey-catching instincts among certain dog breeds, and diverse trajectories of maturity. Dogs, in contrast to their wild counterparts, frequently turn to their human companions for assistance, a characteristic that also influences their distinctive maturation processes.

As we travel through the annals of time, the historical bond between wolves and humans, the symbiosis etched in the evolution of dogs, and the dire resurgence of the Gray wolf unveil a mosaic of resilience and collaboration. These tales become an embodiment of the enduring spirit that transcends challenges, offering a mirror to our capacity for transformation and harmony.

As the last words linger, a plea arises from the ancient forests and the voices of wolves—a call to action. It beckons us to be the stewards of a planet we share, to plant the seeds of empathy, and to foster a world where the dance between nature and humanity is one of balance, understanding, and reverence.

Beyond behavior, physical disparities exist, with wolves generally surpassing dogs in size. Dietary preferences further delineate the 2 species, as wolves lean heavily toward carnivorous habits, primarily consuming meat, while dogs exhibit omnivorous tendencies, capable of digesting both meat and plants.

Taxonomically, dogs are classified as a subspecies of wolves, their domestication spanning millennia. The contrast extends to social structures, where wolves engage in pack dynamics marked by intricate hierarchies; while dogs, by nature, display greater independence and a less complex social structure, relying less on hierarchical dynamics.

This intricate interplay between dogs and humans has sculpted the diverse and distinct behaviors witnessed in our cherished canine companions today, echoing the rich history of their evolution from wolves and the unique imprint left on our hearts by our shared journey through the epochs.

Summary

In the profound tapestry of **"Wolf Women Whisper Wisdom,"** the echoes of nature, the resilience of wolves, and the delicate dance between humanity and the wild reverberate. As we traverse the sacred realms of ancient forests, witness the silent wisdom in a she-wolf's gaze, and ponder the stewardship of our Earth, a chorus of lessons beckons.

In the quiet rustle of leaves and the measured heartbeat of nature, we find the call to humility and understanding. The story unravels a narrative where every creature, from towering trees to majestic wolves, becomes a guardian of profound truths. It urges us to listen to the silent language of trees, the untold stories of wolves, and the collective heartbeat of our shared home.

In reflection of our actions, the story illuminates the urgency of responsible stewardship. The majestic she-wolf, a symbol of rescue and redemption, invites us to question our intrusion into the wild and contemplation of civilization's true meaning. Amidst the clamor of our human existence, it whispers a reminder that the real threat to our environment lies not in the wilderness but in our own hands.

In the whispers of **"Wolf Women Whisper Wisdom,"** we find a story and a guide—an invitation to tread lightly, listen attentively, and embrace the profound interconnectedness that binds us to the wilderness. The lessons embedded in these tales transcend the narrative, becoming beacons of wisdom that challenge us to redefine our relationship with the natural world, encouraging us to step into the role of guardians and listeners in the grand orchestration of life.

Good Puppy Step 7

Select the Perfect Dog Breed

A crucial decision is selecting the right dog breed.

Consider your stage of life, health, lifestyle, financial

capacity, puppy parent educational experience, and

training goals that fit the dog's breed.

Pinecrest Abbey and the Puppy Paradox Letters

In the charming fall countryside, nestled in the heart of the serene setting of Pinecrest Abbey, resided Aria, the Golden Retriever whose wisdom and grace were as enchanting as the forest-covered landscape cloaked in a rainbow of vibrant sunlit fall colors around her. Her name was a melodic ode to the spirit of new beginnings that echoed through the gentle breeze, weaving an intricate tapestry of harmony and warmth. My life is far removed from the bustling city lights and rapid pace. My days are spent amidst 125,000 acres of rolling hills and crisp New England mornings. The daily schedule of activities begins at 8 a.m. sharp.

I am a Canine Concierge, head of security here at Pinecrest Abbey. My job is to alert the staff when the post arrives and sniff letters to find dangerous things concealed. Approximately 300 a day arrive asking Puppy Parent Bootcamp Director Susan E. Lewis for help with their dogs. Then, the letters are delivered in concert with a formal breakfast buffet to the library, where the Canine Concierge staff reads every letter. They carefully sort the inquiries according to the level of urgency. For security reasons, of course, I will not confirm or deny I have taken the liberty to taste-test breakfast before serving. I highly recommend Moms Mix Minimuffins charcuterie board full of warm pumpkin, apple, sweet potato, blueberry, and carrot muffins!

The rainbow of lights reflecting off the sparkling chandeliers ignited the zoomies! The bewildered audience stood frozen, holding fragile crystal glasses, silver teapots, Venectian glass tea sets, serving trays, and stacks of urgent letters! In a flash, I ran 4 laps around the library, jumped over the 2 couches, past a blazing fireplace, under tables, then weaved through the mahogany bookcases and the audience in perfect time to a waltz. Ahh! I caught the blue, yellow, and grey lightning bolts! The handsome Butler, Winston Sterling, calmly glanced at his pocket watch, "25 seconds excellent time this morning, Aria!" The bewildered audience simultaneously held up scorecard "10"!

Winston handed me a silver tray laden with letters, their scents—vanilla, coconut, and the stress emanating from 3 out of 50—wafting in the air. I selected the 3 urgent letters and handed them to Winston. "Excellent, thank you, Aria!" he said before promptly arranging them in a large woven gold basket marked "**Special Delivery—Urgent**" for the Canine Concierge team.

Unbeknownst to me, I dozed off on my back, snoring loudly, captivated by the comforting aromas of vanilla and coconut in front of the glowing fireplace. The baffled Canine Concierges were left listening to the pandemonium that filled the cathedral-ceilinged room. Amused, Winston gently roused me from my slumber.

With an understanding of a thousand words and an adeptness at reading facial expressions, we dogs can detect the essence of a person, be it good or bad, and even alert to medical afflictions. My concern grew as I eavesdropped on the Canine Concierge team interpreting urgent letters from Puppy Parents seeking help with dog training issues.

The paradoxical requests in the Puppy Letters underscored the importance of Good Puppy Step 6: carefully selecting the perfect dog breed. Too often, the root of the problem lies with uneducated or unwise dog Parents, whose life stage, health, lifestyle, financial capacity, educational experience, and training goals become the primary issues, rather than their dog.

My vulnerable canine friends often find themselves trapped in stressful environments due to the paradox that their Parents invite them into situations they cannot manage. This highlights the significance of Good Puppy Step 1: consulting a certified American Kennel Club dog trainer and veterinarian before acquiring a puppy. The human species has developed attention spans shorter than a puppy's, a tendency to lack discernment in important decisions, and a proclivity for ending relationships prematurely.

Dear America's Fairy Dogmother,

I need to schedule an online conference call to discuss the next steps to help our dog, Teddy, a Maltese, and my parents. Both of my parents reside in assisted living due to memory loss. Our small canine companion, Teddy, needs to be trained to use an indoor bathroom. This would be beneficial because it would allow him to relieve himself as needed, reducing the risk of my dad falling during winter outdoor walks. Additionally, there's a concern that they may forget to let Teddy out at night. Although we attempted to use a dog walker, my dad was confused about the walker's presence. I enrolled Teddy and myself in the Puppy Parent Bootcamp online class at **pupppyparentbootcamp.com.**
Sincerely,
Brandy

Dear America's Fairy Dogmother,

Will you grant our wish? Lilly, our energetic Irish Setter, has been part of our family since she was a puppy, and we want her trained as a service dog. Michael, my husband, works with kids with special needs. They would benefit from having our dog become a service dog. Do you think that is a good idea? The students love listening to my husband read Aria's enchanting adventures at Pinecrest Abbey during story time. They wish to learn about the **10 Good Puppy Steps** and meet Aria during the online class: **Puppy Parent Bootcamp**. We went ahead and registered for the class at **puppyparentbootcamp.com**
Thank you!
Rachel

The staff had a go at catching the flying party paper streamers and confetti when I heard my name. My concerned countenance changed to the confident Canine Concierge. Winston had fun playing soccer with me. He quickly glanced at his pocket watch and then brushed my silky red coat. It is almost 11:30 a.m. The staff will read one more letter. Then we will go to deliver the basket of letters to Miss Susan. She is expecting us!

Dear America's Fairy Dogmother,

I hope this message finds you well. I am seeking urgent advice regarding a concerning situation with our two three-year-old dogs. We have recently experienced seven serious dog fights, and the tension at home has made me extremely anxious.

My husband is suggesting the drastic measure of putting them down, but I am exploring alternative options such as training and rehoming. I am reaching out to you for guidance on whether this could be a wise decision for our dogs, considering our limited budget.

One of our dogs displays severe aggression, while the other can be aggressive in specific circumstances despite having an overall easy-going attitude. Recognizing our mistake in not properly socializing or training them as puppies, we have taken the initiative to enroll in the Puppy Parent Bootcamp at puppyparentbootcamp.com. This program seems to be affordable and might provide the training and support our dogs need.

I am desperate to find a solution that does not involve putting our beloved pets down. I would greatly appreciate your insights and advice on whether training and rehoming could be a viable and compassionate option.

Thank you for taking the time to consider our situation. I look forward to hearing from you soon.

Sincerely,
Crystal

Winston whisked away the basket off the desk and gave it to me to carry. He glanced at his pocket watch once more. "Come along, Miss Aria, it is time to deliver the letters!"

Summary

"Pinecrest Abbey and the Puppy Paradox Letters" follows Aria, a wise and graceful Golden Retriever, amidst the serene landscapes of Pinecrest Abbey, where she serves as the Canine Concierge and head of security. This countryside has received 300 letters daily, seeking guidance from Puppy Parent Bootcamp Director Susan Lewis. Aria and her team meticulously sort through these letters, identifying urgent pleas from dog owners facing various training and behavioral challenges.

As Aria maneuvers through her duties, she displays incredible agility, racing through the Abbey's library during a chaos-inducing episode, deftly collecting urgent letters. However, her playful nature occasionally leads her to doze off in front of the fireplace, much to the staff's amusement.

The letters themselves reveal the complexities of dog ownership. Brandy seeks assistance training Teddy, a small canine companion, to use an indoor bathroom due to her parents' memory loss. Rachel hopes to transform her Irish Setter, Lilly, into a service dog to aid her husband's work with special-needs children. When facing the heart-wrenching prospect of dog aggression, Crystal seeks advice on training or rehoming her beloved pets.

Throughout the story, the letters highlight the significance of responsible ownership and proper training, emphasizing the bond between humans and their furry friends. Aria's keen understanding of human expressions and emotions allows her to empathize with pet owners' challenges.

The tale showcases the dedication of pet owners and the crucial role Aria and her team play in offering guidance, support, and recommendations, ensuring that each dog receives the best possible care. The story unfolds as a poignant exploration of the intricate relationships between humans and their canine companions, set against the backdrop of Pinecrest Abbey's enchanting landscapes.

Good Puppy Step 8

Learn How to Acquire a Dog Responsibly

HOPE Help One Puppy Every Day

- Support animal shelters and rescue organizations by adopting a dog.
- Save lives by providing a loving home to a dog in need.
- Consider visiting your local shelter or rescue to find your new companion.

Pinecrest Abbey and the Sapphire of Secrets

Chapter 1: HOPE for the Holidays

Aria, the Golden Retriever, lived in the heart of Pinecrest Abbey, nestled within a serene coastal estate. Her presence mirrored the vibrant fall landscape that enveloped the charming seaside property, painting the scenery in hues of warmth and tranquility. Aria's name embodies the hope and potential of fresh starts; her very being sways with the soft breeze, weaving harmony throughout every nook and cranny.

As anticipation for the annual HOPE for the Holidays grew, the estate was excited. Winston Sterling, the distinguished butler, received letters from the mail carrier, accompanied by Aria, the Golden Retriever. Housekeepers adorned the estate with holiday decorations while the kitchen buzzed with activity. General, the mischievous German Shepherd, stole a baked chicken and dashed off playfully.

The flustered red-headed chef, Miss Orla Murphy, named all the saints and the Holy Family while chasing him. Miss Murphy thought she had General cornered at the bottom of a double spiral staircase. Amused by the weekly caper, Winston rescued General again. "Ah, Miss Murphy, a word about the HOPE for the Holidays Masque Ball menu." Orla's name means treasure or golden lady. Seriously, she had more cents in the bank than she did in her head!

Orla, paralyzed by Winston's smile, saw pink hearts and green clovers, while General thought the chicken was magically delicious! With a slight flick of Winston's hand, the 100-pound dog suddenly disappeared through a secret wooden door to the library. The mahogany-carved paneled door told the true story of the midnight voyage of the Whydah Gally in 1717.

The Midnight Voyage of the Whydah Gally

In the ocean's embrace, the Whydah Gally sailed, bound by trade winds, her course unveiled. From London's docks to the African shore, she bore her cargo, rich and more.

Sir Humphry Morice's commissioned pride, named for Whydah, where enslaved people were tied, was a vessel armed, a merchant's scheme to reap the riches of a darkened dream.

Through coastal waves, she ventured far, with gold and enslaved people in her bizarre holds. From Africa's grasp to the Caribbean's might, she traded wares day and night.

Yet fate's design, with a pirate's sway, brought Bellamy's flag on that fateful day. Black Sam's crew, in a daring flight, seized the Whydah Gally on a stormy night.

From trading ship to a pirate's might, her cannons roared in the moon's pale light. With sails full set for the colonies' sight, she charted a course through the ocean's bite.

The winds were unkind, and the tempest's wail unleashed their fury, a merciless gale. Cape Cod's coast, a fearsome host, was where Whydah met her untimely boast.

In the heart of night, the tempest stirred; a nor'easter's wrath, its fury incurred. Gales from the east, the northeast's fierce wail, forcing the Whydah close to a perilous trail
.

Near Cape Cod's shoals, the breaking waves roared. A dance with danger, where fate was scored. Marconi Beach, where destiny drew near, the ship's fate sealed as the storm drew severe.

At midnight's hour, a sandbar embraced the vessel's bow in waters displaced. Sixteen feet deep, just a stone's throw from shore's safety where wild winds blow.

With winds at seventy, a fierce onslaught, and waves towering high, their power was sought. Thirty to forty, in their towering might, engulfed the ship in the storm's cruel fight.

The main mast snapped a thunderous sound, pulling the ship where depths abound. Thirty feet under, in the ocean's grasp, she capsized fast in the tempest's rasp.

Silver and gold, cannons, and crew plunged to depths where the sea's hue grew. Sixty cannons, a destructive force, tore through the ship on a lethal course.

Broken apart in the storm's cruel hand, scattered debris along the coastline's strand: a mournful echo, a tragic tale of a ship lost in the storm's fierce gale.

Survivors few, amidst the debris, bear witness to the violent spree. Thomas Davis, in his trial's light, recalled the horror of that fateful night.

"In a quarter-hour," he solemnly swore, "The mainmast was gone, the ship no more. By morning's light, she was shattered, her story told, her fate, unflattered."

Torn asunder by the raging sea's breath, she sank below, embracing death. Her treasure scattered, her crew astray, lost in the depths where the wreckage lay.

Centuries passed, her secrets buried 'neath sand, in an ocean's shroud. 'til Clifford's quest, with map in hand, Unveiled her resting on the seabed's sand.

The Whydah Gally's 1716 bell that chimed in the ship's proud prime now told her tale through the waves of time. Artifacts reclaimed, a story told, of pirates bold and the ship's stronghold.

In Provincetown's halls, her relics displayed the Whydah's legacy, never to fade. A tale of fortune, of stormy fate, In history's ledger, her chapter's weight.
Among the wreckage, a poignant trace—a child's shoe—was found in that watery space. It is a story untold of a youthful plea, lost in the annals of the deep, the sea.

Whydah Gally, a vessel's lore, a tale of adventure, forevermore. In sunken depths, her story thrives, captured in time, where history dives.

Authored by: Susan Elizabeth Lewis

Meanwhile, in the Library Labyrinth Lore, the Canine Concierge team diligently wrote letters and opened applications from Dog Scent Work finalists. The real winners of the competition are the hundreds of dogs adopted at the HOPE for the Holidays event, finding forever homes. It is a magical time of year when what is lost becomes found.

The enigmatic 18th-century gentleman depicted in a regal portrait puzzled everyone except Aria. His elegant stature and a bejeweled cane adorned with an immense sapphire held a valuable secret unbeknownst to the staff—a hidden treasure map concealed within the cane, leading to the undiscovered pirate treasure of 400,000 gold coins. The enigmatic tale of the vanished Sapphire of Secrets lingered within the invisible pages of an ancient leather-bound, illuminated valuable book hidden in the Library Labyrinth Lore. It is history, murmuring cryptic codes, elusive clues, and age-old riddles.

Away from the bustling city lights, Pinecrest Abbey offered a haven embraced by the inviting sea breeze and a sprawling 150-mile estate. Here, daily life commenced promptly at 8 a.m. Aria, the Canine Concierge and head of security, took her responsibilities seriously. Her duties involved alerting the staff upon mail arrival and meticulously sniffing letters to uncover concealed threats, ensuring the estate and its inhabitants' safety.

Aria's and General's canine noses subtly emerge from beneath the breakfast buffet tablecloth. Of course, for security purposes, I can neither confirm nor deny that General and I indulged in a pre-service taste-test of the breakfast spread. Allow me to earnestly endorse the delightful assortment of Mom's Mix Minimuffins, a charming charcuterie board boasting warm flavors of pumpkin, apple, sweet potato, blueberry, and carrot muffins!

Meanwhile, my friend General seemed quite content with the succulent roast chicken he acquired from the kitchen. Not content with just that, he made off with a few unidentified, irresistibly fuzzy socks and a peculiar black pirate costume glove that reeked of strong beer and smoke—a scent that did not quite sit well with me. There appeared to be an object hidden inside about the size of my favorite toy, a tennis ball. But, as they say, General's mom did not raise a fool; his keen police dog instincts detected something amiss, leading him to carefully conceal his newfound treasures beneath the table.

Winston, observing from a distance, found amusement in General's stealthy maneuvers, snatching socks without the Pinecrest guests noticing their disappearance. It seemed like a clever game, with people wandering about, unknowingly missing a sock or two. Winston saw this as an opportunity to assist General in honing his skills for the HOPE for the Holidays Scent Work Championship.

Winston glanced at the 24k-gold pocket watch he inherited from his great-grandfather, remarking at General's impeccable timing. "Excellent, 15 seconds!" The family heirloom is adorned with engravings and an inscription from the Victorian era. Timepieces once symbolized grace and distinction among the elite. Unbeknownst to him, this watch held a key that would unlock a mystery at the Scent Work Championship at Pinecrest Abbey.

Winston's large pocket watch and locket, engraved with the Pinecrest family seal, concealed a cryptic inscription behind a bejeweled locket door adorned with a woman's photo.

> "In moments lost to history's shroud,
> where sails met storm and secrets vowed,
> Guide to treasures underneath the sea's span,
> the map concealed in Pirate's hand.
> Seek not the gem kings adore but the fortune for those in lore.
> By canine wit and wisdom's key,
> uncover what's lost in history's decree."

This inscription hints at the hidden treasure map concealed within the Pirate's cane, leading to the undiscovered wealth—a crucial clue to solving the mystery of the vanished Sapphire of Secrets!

Chapter 2: Masquerade of Masters Ball

Once a year, Pinecrest Abbey opened its doors to a peculiar event that combined elegance, artistry, and a noble cause: the Masquerade of Masters Ball. It was a night when guests transcended the ordinary, transforming into living works of art from fine art masterpieces. Guests froze still for a moment, then suddenly came to life by stepping out of the staged paintings. Amidst the opulent affair, with my canine friends adorned in their finest, it was an evening of sophistication and purpose, marked by the annual Hope for the Holidays dog adoption and Dog Scent Work Championship.

The tranquil night shattered when a red-headed thief, masquerading as the pirate depicted in the life-size 18th-century masterpiece hung in the Library Labyrinth Lore, attempted to pilfer the Sapphire of Secrets, replacing it with a glass imitation. But fate had different plans, for Aria, the astute Golden Retriever head of security, sensed deception.

Accompanied by General, my companion German Shepherd and former police dog, we unearthed the truth. Clad in one glove, the other pilfered by General, containing the true Sapphire of Secrets, the Canine Crusaders held the key to foiling the thief's plan!

As chaos ensued, a comical chase unfurled. The thief pursued General and me, zoomie-weaving through the human agility course, across the ballroom and into the formal dining room. Bewildered servers caught dishes and platters. Winston caught flying fruit cakes with the grace of a quarterback. I jumped over a couch and caught a flying roast chicken! Laughter mingled with suspense as the daring chase navigated the lavish corridors of Pinecrest Abbey.

Amidst the frantic pursuit, I recalled the telltale scent of beer and smoke emanating from the pilfered glove. General, the unwitting accomplice, carried the treasure, oblivious to its worth, while the frustrated thief named all the saints and the Holy Family. The thief's determined strides echoed behind the double staircase. General and I ran up the staircase, hid behind a curtain, and waited for the exhausted thief to catch up. I barked the order! "OK, General, push the button now!" Suddenly, the staircase transformed into a slide, and the thief slid down just in time to get stuck on top of the 35-foot artificial Christmas tree rapidly rising through the basement-floor elevator shaft while the audience crooned carols!

The Abbey reverberated with canine determination and human laughter, a whirlwind of furry heroism and human antics as we raced to safeguard the treasure and uphold the Abbey's legacy.

In a moment of whimsical triumph, Chef Orla Murphy was apprehended, and the Sapphire of Secrets was restored to its rightful hiding place, leaving Pinecrest Abbey enveloped in the joyous echoes of a memorable, albeit chaotic, Masquerade of Masters Ball.

Chapter 3: The HOPE for the Holidays Dog Scent Work Competition

The crisp morning air enveloped Pinecrest Abbey as the estate geared up for the prestigious HOPE for the Holidays Dog Scent Work competition. General William Kingston, Winston Sterling, and I, adorned in our finest, stood among a group of eager participants and their canine companions.

Aria, the Golden Retriever, exuded confidence as the head of security, but today, she was more than that. She was Winston's trusted ally, and General's acute senses complemented their team perfectly. They proudly sport their team's name, the Canine Crusaders, and the Pinecrest Abbey green and gold colors. They studied the Secret Sniffer Scavenger Hunt map listing seven hidden items in four locations: the Winter Woodland Wonderland, Candy Cane Lane, Library Labyrinth Lore, and Bishops Brig Bell Tower. The other two teams competing, the blue Bark Brigade and burgundy Rescue Rangers Secret Sniffer Scavenger Hunt team maps pointed to four separate locations at Pinecrest Abbey, where seven different items were hidden to ensure the dogs experienced only fun and success!

The Bark Brigade returned to defend their two-year winning streak. Mr. Trevor Branagan; his daughter Miss Bonney Branagan; and their dogs—Irish Setter Molly and Beagle Bailey—were jolly competitors and dear friends of Pinecrest Abbey. Winston was always amused listening to Mr. Branagan proudly telling the story of his dogs' Scent Work competition victories. After drinking a pint or two of Pinecrest Panache, the stories became grander, larger-than-life legends.

"In Pinecrest Abbey's grand scent-seeking race,
brave teams set the woodland's swift pace.
With hounds by their side and spirits allied,
they hunt hidden treasures, a chase!
My daughter Bonney, with laughter and cheer,
recited, her voice ringing clear,
"In search of the prize, with stars in our eyes,
Bark Brigade, hold victory near!"

Authored by: Susan Elizabeth Lewis

The professional Rescue Rangers team of Giorgina and Valentina Mariano strategically studied the Secret Sniffer Scavenger Hunt team map that pointed to four separate locations at Pinecrest Abbey, where seven different items were hidden. The fierce female force of furry friends—Fancy, a Labrador Retriever, and Flame, a Redbone Coonhound—were excited to start! The Boston-proper, wicked-smart sisters' brains and beauty would prove to be a distracting match for Winston Sterling at the dinner party celebration. The Rescue Rangers, sporting burgundy uniforms, were seasoned competitors known to execute Scent Work competitions with military precision.

The competition's challenges were as intricate as the mysteries they often encountered, weaving through the Abbey's sprawling grounds, rich with aromatic hideaways. Our team, the Canine Crusaders, synchronized in purpose and set off on the first leg of the competition. Winston, usually composed, felt a surge of excitement mixed with a dash of anticipation. His pocket watch gently swung from his vest pocket, the family crest glinting in the morning sunlight, a silent reminder of the quest ahead. William, the General's dad, was a forest ranger who worked at Pinecrest Abbey. His cautious nature, woodland skills, and sense of direction proved invaluable scent work skills for the quest.

As we maneuvered through the wooded trails, I heard the echo of the Abbey's Bishop's Brig Bell Tower in the distance. We stumbled upon the Library Labyrinth Lore, one of the checkpoints in the competition. The old library held a magnetic allure, drawing us in with its air of mystery. My keen sense picked up a subtle scent lingering around the bookshelves, a smell I had encountered before—the enigmatic aroma of hidden clues.

Without hesitation, Winston, William, General, and I ventured inside towards a cozy fireplace. The regal paintings adorning the walls seemed to gaze down upon us as if silently urging us onward. But the beautiful, ancient, embossed gold book, with its blank pages, beckoned Winston closer. As Winston opened the codex titled **The Sapphire of Secrets**, the pages filled with cryptic messages and riddles, words appearing and vanishing in sync with their intent to solve the Sapphire of Secrets mystery. The book responded to Winston's honest questions and strength of faith, guiding him with invisible ink and whispered clues.

General's acute sense of smell guided us to a hidden corner of the Library Labyrinth Lore. A painting revealed a pirate holding a compass in his left hand and an engraved bejeweled cane, the Sapphire of Secrets-crowned cane, secretly concealing The Bishop's Brig treasure map in his right hand. I noticed Winston carried the same compass, a family air loom in his left hand. As Winston held it, the compass spun wildly, aligning with clues from the book and hidden inscription inside his dual-purpose pocket watch and locket.

With the painting acting as a secret vault, the real cane and Sapphire of Secrets stone gleamed laser beams in the firelight. General and I reminded ourselves not to get the zoomies! Our team, the Canine Crusaders, now more synchronized than ever, followed the compass's erratic dance through the woods surrounding Pinecrest Abbey.

Winston's calmness contrasted sharply with William's nervous energy. Amidst the twists and turns of the wooded trail, Winston's composed demeanor proved invaluable, keeping us focused and resilient. Progressing deeper into the woods, deciphering clues and riddles, the forest seemed to aid our earnest quest.

We approached a hidden clearing at the Bishop's Brig Bell Tower dated 1776. Below, in a cave, lay the resting place of the Bishop's pirate treasure chest—400,000 gold coins. Once fastened to The Bishop, the bell sank in 1776 off Cape Cod's coast when a fierce nor' easter snapped the brig in two.

The sinking ship rolled over and spilled one hundred tons of treasure into the sea. The Bishop's bow remained visible at low tide inside the cave. The portrait of Thomas Sterling, Winston Sterling's great-grandfather, forced into piracy, survived the wreck, and took the Sapphire of Secrets, pocket watch, compass, bejeweled cane, and treasure map with him.

Aria, General, Winston, and William, united by an unforeseen journey and unwavering camaraderie, unearthed The Bishop's treasure that had eluded seekers for centuries. With the compass pointing them back home, they headed back to Pinecrest Abbey, their hearts filled with the satisfaction of solving the Sapphire of Secrets mystery and a newfound sense of kinship forged through their shared adventure.

The Canine Crusaders gracefully withdrew from the competition, acknowledging the indispensable role of canine-assisted scent work in solving the mystery. As the Bark Brigade and Rescue Rangers raced for the final item, the Rescue Rangers emerged victorious, marking a jubilant end to the event that saw 500 dogs finding forever homes.

Good Puppy Step 8: Learn to acquire a dog responsibly.
HOPE Help One Puppy Every Day

- Support animal shelters and rescue organizations by adopting dogs.
- Save lives by providing a loving home to a dog in need.
- Consider visiting your local shelter or rescue to find your new companion.

Summary

In **"Pinecrest Abbey and the Sapphire of Secrets,"** the story begins with the tranquil setting of Pinecrest Abbey, where the anticipation for the annual HOPE for the Holidays event grows. Amidst holiday preparations and the bustling activities at the estate, an enigmatic tale unfolds. Aria, the Golden Retriever; Winston, the butler; and General, the mischievous German Shepherd, find themselves entangled in a historical mystery surrounding the vanished Sapphire of Secrets.

The storyline traces back to the 18th-century voyage of the Whydah Gally, a ship laden with treasures that met a tragic fate off Cape Cod's coast. The intriguing history intertwines with present-day events, including a thief's attempt to steal the Sapphire during the Masquerade of Masters Ball.

The narrative takes an adventurous turn with the HOPE for the Holidays Dog Scent Work competition. Teams, including the Canine Crusaders led by Aria, General, Winston, and William, embark on a quest filled with cryptic clues and hidden treasures. Through their canine instincts and teamwork, they decode riddles, uncover secrets hidden in the Library Labyrinth Lore, and ultimately discover The Bishop's long-lost pirate treasure.

The tale emphasizes unity, the bond between humans and dogs, and the importance of supporting animal shelters and rescues. Amidst historical intrigue and heartwarming adventures, the story resonates with the spirit of hope, camaraderie, and the significance of finding loving homes for dogs in need.

Good Puppy Step 9

Explore the Responsibilities of Dog Ownership and Animal Welfare Laws

- Vaccination Requirements
- Licensing and Identification Procedures
- Prevention of Animal Cruelty
- Leash Regulations (Excluding Choke, Prong, or E-Collars)
- Spaying and Neutering Laws for Adult Dogs (1 year - 18 month old)

Chapter 1

In the heart of Pinecrest Abbey, a sanctuary nestled within the sprawling landscape of New England, the annual Grove Giving Gala stood as a beacon of significance. This vibrant event wasn't merely a dazzling spectacle but a profound reminder of stewardship towards nature and wildlife conservation. It echoed the fundamental values of reforesting and preserving the beauty surrounding the Abbey's 150,000-acre forest. At the heart of this extraordinary tale lay the incredible partnership between the Canine Crusaders Security Team and the humans who diligently upheld animal welfare laws, embodying the essence of responsible pet ownership. Their unity symbolized a commitment to safeguarding the environment and its inhabitants.

Aquila, the majestic Bald eagle soaring above Pinecrest Abbey's landscape, epitomized resilience, embodying the triumph of the Bald eagle's resurgence from near extinction. Her story mirrored the endangered status of these magnificent creatures in the 20th century, nearly wiped out due to human actions. The 70,000 Bald eagles shot in New York during the 1930s served as a poignant reminder of the dangerous brink they faced. However, Aquila's soaring flight above the Abbey represented a success story—a testament to what happens when humanity honors the responsibility bestowed upon them, echoing the teachings of Genesis 2:15. The Abbey, akin to the Garden of Eden and Noah's Ark, served as a haven where life flourished under the careful stewardship of its residents.

In the bustling halls of Pinecrest Abbey, amidst the anticipation of the Grove Giving Gala, a tale unfolded, intertwining the echoes of the past with the present. Sarah Kidd's resilience and unwavering spirit reflected the tenacity needed to navigate life's trials, mirroring the journey of the Bald Eagles from the brink of extinction to national symbol status. The Gala's glittering atmosphere during the festive 1920s hinted at the Abbey's commitment to preserving the environment while celebrating its history. The Abbey, with all its intrigue and glamour, served as a living proof of how humans, animals, and nature can coexist in harmony, creating a beautiful and vibrant tapestry of life. As the story unfolded with Aquila's daring escapades and the alliance between humans and animals, it encapsulated the essence of conservation, responsibility, and the unwavering spirit to protect and nurture the environment —lessons echoing through time within the walls of Pinecrest Abbey.

Aquila, the Bald eagle, gracefully soared over Pinecrest Abbey's sprawling landscape, her 6-foot wingspan catching the crisp September Atlantic Ocean breeze. She circled the familiar tree where she'd hatched, reminiscing about the day puppy Aria and forester William Kingston discovered her with a broken wing.

Aria and William encountered her distress as her mother anxiously trailed Winston's truck to the Pinecrest Abbey Wildlife Veterinary Hospital. With his gentle demeanor, he tried to calm the frightened eaglet while her father stayed in the nest with her brother, his worry evident in his protective stance. Kind and cautious, William formed an unexpected bond with Aquila, aiding her rehabilitation and eventual release into the wild. Surprisingly, the Canine Crusade security team formed a unique friendship, engaging in playful games of chase and fetch with the intelligent eagle.

Aquila's exceptional vision and acute hearing contributed to her remarkable intelligence, enabling her to process information swiftly and accurately. Winston Sterling installed a Squawk Box at the Forest Ranger Station and Pinecrest Abbey, allowing Aquila to signal danger or aid to animals and people in need, solidifying her role as a guardian of the land.

Under the guidance of General, the retired police dog, Aquila developed a mischievous streak. Dubbed "**Artful Talon**," she delighted in playfully stealing, hiding, and guarding food and shiny treasures. She even partook in a hilarious kitchen caper, hiding in vaulted ceiling beams while General raided the refrigerator, causing chaos among the kitchen staff.

Spotting a fish breakfast from afar while circling the ocean, Aquila dived from a great height at nearly 100 miles per hour, showcasing her impressive hunting prowess. As she soared around Pinecrest Abbey, anticipation for the upcoming Harvest Grove Giving Gala tingled within her. The vibrant fall leaf colors of the 150,000-acre forest resembled a rainbow of confetti, painting the landscape with autumn hues. Among the scenery, she spotted her dear friends Winston Sterling and Aria collecting mail at the open front door. With excitement, Aquila swooped down for a visit, playfully engaging Aria in a game of "fetch the flying letters," sending the startled postman scrambling for safety.

In the bustling halls of Pinecrest Abbey, an unexpected visitor sent hearts racing and plans tumbling like a house of cards. Aquila, the majestic Bald Eagle with eyes that could pierce the heavens, spied a top-secret, glimmering gold package clasped in Winston's hand. The Artful Talon couldn't resist its allure and swooped down, ignorant of its immense value.

Winston, always prepared for the unexpected, flashed his 24k gold-inscribed pocket watch—the same watch that unraveled the enigma of the Sapphire of Secrets and unearthed the elusive Bishop's Brig treasure, hidden for centuries.

Aquila bolted, flying through the Abbey's entrance and perching atop a towering 35-foot artificial pine tree, startling the staff adorning it with tree-planting donations for the upcoming Grove Giving Gala. Negotiations ensued, with Aria, ever the diplomatic companion, dashing off to beseech Mrs. Bridget O'Connell, Pinecrest Abbey's new Master Chef, for fish to barter for the prized package.

Aria's insistent bark and fish-fetching antics coaxed Mrs. O'Connell into an unexpected confrontation with Aquila. The formidable bird dove toward her, relinquishing the package to seize the fish. "Bejaysus and begorrah!" Mrs. O'Connell's exclamation echoed through the Abbey. "Holy St. Patrick! Why is there a Bald eagle in the house?" gasped she, bewildered by the spectacle.

Amidst laughter, Winston apologized, and a composed Mrs. O'Connell calmly retrieved the secretive parcel. Quickly easing the tension, the dashing butler extended a silver serving tray adorned with crystal glasses filled with Pinecrest Panache. "Perhaps a swig or two to calm my nerves," she mused. "That bird gave me such a start. I nearly left my heart back at the stove!"

As the majestic eagle, Aquila, continued to grace Pinecrest Abbey with her daring flights and playful escapades, her bold adventures often echoed the tales of another figure who left an indelible mark on history. Centuries earlier, amidst the windswept shores of New England, a woman named Sarah Kidd forged her path, navigating the turbulent seas of life's trials and adventures. Her true story, one of resilience and unwavering New England spirit, intertwined with the legends of daring voyages and hidden treasures, captivating hearts with echoes of the past.

With a slight flick of Winston's hand, the mysterious glittering gold package suddenly disappeared through a secret wooden door to Bounty Booty Brig. The mahogany-carved paneled door told the true story of New England's Pirate Queen Sarah and Captain William Kidd, who married in May 1691.

New England's Pirate Queen Sarah Kidd

In Captain Kidd's Wife Sarah, a tale of resilience and might, four unions, each bearing its plight. Widowed thrice in life's endless game, yet from the shadows, she carved her name.

From England's shores, her journey began amidst marriages and loss, a steadfast plan. Tangled in Kidd's nor'easter storm, a tempest brews, yet she emerged strong, her spirit infused.

Accused by association, suspicion's shroud, Her husband's pursuits, her life unbowed. Lord Bellomont's hand, a tightening hold, in shadows of doubt, her story told.

Locked in chains of unjust despair, her innocence questioned, her rights laid bare. Yet in the face of adversity's cruel jest, she weathered the nor'easter storm, her soul at rest.

Released from the grasp of wrongful blame, her possessions restored, her spirit aflame. A new chapter unfurled in New York's embrace, Sarah charted her course, a resilient grace.

While Captain Kidd faced fate's relentless chase, in London's gallows, his final place, Sarah, undeterred, crafted anew; a tavern opened, and dreams pursued true.

With earnings from past unions' traces, her legacy thrived in that tavern's space. A woman of strength reinvented and free, Sarah Kidd is a testament to resilience, you see.

In my heart's lament, I, Sarah Bradley Cox Oort, my tailspin a yarn of fateful strides. Thrice wedded, then a fourth's embrace, In life's bounds, a fortune's trace.

Stone Prison's grip, a cold despair, Where my husband, Captain William Kidd, in silence, bare. His whispered words, in silent night's embrace, Echoes through bars in endless chase.

Boston's betrayal and chains did bind Stone Prison's cold, tormented mind. Awaiting trial in Newgate's keep, Kidd faced fate in silence deep.

Oh, the coast we sailed, New England's shore, Battling ships, and tempests' roar: Kidd's quest, a treasure's lore, Midst Cape Cod's tales of rich folklore.

I, a lady bound to wed, with limited choices in my path and no learning's light nor freedoms, spread **life** in the corset's warring thread.

Captain Kidd's Adventure Galley sails unfurled and bore down the waves, a nautical world. But as storms raged and dreams whirled, our destinies swirled in fate's grip.

Marrying wealth, my only course, lacked education, a silent force. Bound by law, as was the source, A woman's life, a limited course.

On December 4, 1700, back in 95, Adventure Galley, she came alive. A sleek and strong vessel, her sails embraced the winds, her oars controlled. She was more than wood, more than mere steel, a venture of dreams and pirate's zeal.

Bought for my husband's quest by backers bold, to reclaim plunder and fortunes untold. I watched her rise from deep waters, the marriage of sails, an oar-powered sweep. Her hull, a question, her strength untried, would she conquer seas or in them? From London's port, she sailed with grace, the my captain's hope, an eager chase.

Yet winds of fate blew off their course, no pirate's catch, just trials and remorse. Across the oceans, on waves, she strayed, to distant lands, her prow displayed. But luck did not favor, nor treasure guide, her hull weakened; her destiny untied.

In Madagascar's haven, her fate was cast, leaky and worn, her time surpassed. Stripped of her worth, sunk to the deep, Adventure Galley rests in eternal sleep. The echoes remain of a ship renowned, once sought treasures, now legends crowned. A Pirate Queen's Tale, with a wife's lament, of a vessel lost, her journey meant.

In June 1699, my husband Captain Kidd, a tale he weaved, On Gardiners Island, secrets he cleaved. With a chest of gold and silver's sheen, In a ravine, his treasures unseen.

Permission sought, and a box for Bellomont, Kidd did declare. To Mrs. Gardiner, gifts to bear, gold cloth and sugar, his thanks to share. A legend spun a dire threat, Yet Kidd's demeanor bore no fret. Civil and calm, his conduct met, As history's pen recalls, I bet.

Trials in Boston, orders proclaimed, Governor's request, treasure reclaimed. Gold dust, silver bars, jewels unnamed, A trove of riches, tales acclaimed.

Diamonds, rubies, candle's light, Gardiner's keep, a daughter's delight. A plaque now stands as a testament right where Kidd's treasure lay, out of sight.

Authored by: Susan Elizabeth Lewis

Chapter 2 The Tune Raiders

Isabella Bianchi, Luca De Rosa, Marco Santoro, and Giovanni Moretti, the quartet of grifters, hailed from the vibrant Italian community in Boston's North End in this tightly knit enclave where family, food, and traditions intertwined seamlessly. At the heart of this community stood Maria Moretti, Giovanni's grandmother, an immigrant from Italy, whose bakery, the famed Maria's Bakery, served as a hub of activity and the nucleus of neighborhood news.

Every afternoon, between 12:00 and 3:00, families congregated at Maria's Bakery, engaging in spirited games of bocce, exchanging stories, and relishing Maria's delectable pastries. Laughter and camaraderie filled the bustling establishment while the delicious scent of freshly baked goods wafted through the air.

Maria Moretti, a respected and wealthy figure within the community, received a formal invitation to the annual Grove Giving Gala from the Canine Concierge team at Pinecrest Abbey. The gold seal embossed with the image of Aquila, the Bald eagle symbolizing conservation and reforestation, graced the envelope—a subtle nod to Maria's longstanding support of Pinecrest Abbey's initiatives, a fact kept discreet from most.

Unbeknownst to Maria, the quartet of Isabella, Luca, Marco, and Giovanni, individuals she had watched grow up, were also plotting their attendance at the same Gala with a very different agenda—to steal the prized Pinecrest Abbey Emerald and orchestrate its auction overseas through Isabella's connections.

Isabella Bianchi, the captivating singer with emerald-green eyes, possessed intellect and cunning, leveraging her expertise in art and business to navigate the world of cons and auctions. Her roots intertwined with Luca De Rosa, the flamboyant pianist known as the Tune Raider, whose handsome charm and musical prowess attracted women like a magnet. However, his knack for getting entangled in affairs led to several legal issues.

Marco Santoro, the reserved and scholarly trumpet player, harbored a depth of knowledge in technology, code, and safe-cracking, his mind a repository of information and strategies. Supported by Maria Moretti after losing his parents, Marco's quiet demeanor masked his exceptional skills.

Giovanni Moretti, the black sheep of his family, mastered the art of deception within Maria's reputable bakery, his proficiency in jewelry and pastry craftsmanship used for less-than-legal ventures. His grandmother's influence loomed large, a fear of her wrath a constant presence in his life, alongside his phobias of birds and dogs and his addiction to smoking.

Chapter 3 The Grifters

In the exhilarating world of Pinecrest Abbey during the optimistic 1920s, the echoes of jazz reverberated through hidden speakeasies and clandestine gatherings. These elusive establishments were the beating heart of a Prohibition-era society, where the clinking of glasses and hushed murmurs of patrons formed the symphony of the night.

The reforesting Grove Giving Gala was a spectacle of charm and allure, a dazzling event set against the backdrop of flappers dancing to jazz melodies and gentlemen exuding an air of mystique in their sleek suits. However, four grifters were hidden beneath the glitz and glamour, poised to enact their tale of illusion amid the revelry.

The curtains were drawn back to reveal Pinecrest Abbey's "Mystery Night" at the Giving Grove Gala, an annual event dedicated to reforesting. The spotlight fell on the surprise play titled "The Grifters." Isabella Bianchi, the enchanting, sultry jazz singer with captivating green eyes, stumbled upon whispers of this unfolding drama courtesy of an overzealous manicurist in Boston's North End. She read about her old college flame, Winston Sterling, and the Pinecrest Emerald Cross necklace. Her resolve to become the next Pirate Queen of New England was unshakable.

In the effervescent realm of Pinecrest Abbey, a spectacular event unfolded—the annual Grove Giving Gala. Amidst the glitz and glamour, the quartet of grifters—Isabella, Luca, Marco, and Giovanni—crafted their ambitious plan to lay their hands on the coveted Pinecrest Abbey Emerald Cross necklace, unaware of a looming surprise.

The Canine Crusaders heroes, alongside Mr. Trevor Branagan, Boston's esteemed detective, always remained a thorn in their side. But little did they know, the most unforeseen twist awaited them in the form of Mama Maria, the beloved figure from their childhood, the formidable force of the North End.

The Gala buzzed with excitement, masked by an air of intrigue as party goers reveled in the festivities. Unbeknownst to the grifters, the Pinecrest Abbey Emerald took center stage not just as a prized possession but also as a replica of high-quality costume jewelry distributed as party favors to the guests, a memento of the illustrious affair.

As the night waltzed on, Isabella, Luca, Marco, and Giovanni maneuvered through the opulent venue, their eyes fixated on the supposed Emerald, envisioning a successful heist that would secure their fortunes. But fate had its twisted sense of humor in store for them.

Disguised as the headline band, "The Speakeasy Swing Trio," these cunning grifters had slyly infiltrated the Gala. Their facade as performers granted them unfettered access to the Abbey's corridors, shrouded by the dazzling aura of the event.

As the night unfolded, the band took the stage, their melodies serving as a smokescreen for their covert agenda and strategically positioning them near Winston Sterling's exhibit of the Bishop's Brig treasure of historical artifacts and the famed Pinecrest Emerald Cross necklace, which was a copy for security reasons.

While the guests reveled in the music and spectacle, unbeknownst to them, the grifters had pored over archaic maps and cryptic tomes, uncovering the Abbey's hidden passages and secret compartments. Their singular aim was the Pinecrest Emerald necklace—a treasure shimmering with priceless gems. Marco Santoro discovered how to open the Bounty Booty Brig, where the genuine Pinecrest Abbey Emerald necklace was concealed. Aquila guarded the vault perched on her favorite spot, the 35-foot Grove Giving Tree adorned with donations.

Trusting Mrs. O'Malley, the master chef hired Mama Maria's grandson Giovanni, a master pastry chef, to make two cakes for the event. He learned how to open the Bounty Booty Brig from his code-cracker friend Marco, who forgot to tell him how to turn off the security camera inside the vault. Giovanni made two three-tier Surprise Cakes.

He took the genuine Pinecrest Emerald and hid it inside one of the cakes. Smoking was not allowed at Pinecrest Abbey. Aria and General, scent work champions, did not like the smell of smoke. Nervous about the heist, Giovanni smoked a cigarette near the cakes. Then he forgot which cake the necklace was hidden in. The Surprise Cakes were identical. He hoped to escape unnoticed while the Speakeasy Swing Trio and Isabella's sultry voice and emerald eyes hypnotized the audience and Winson. Fate had other plans.

Meanwhile, Aria, General, and Aquila engaged in an unexpected yet uproarious chase around the Abbey. Giovanni, by mistake, rolled out the Suprise Cake containing the genuine Pinecrest Emerald that smelled like cigarette smoke. Giovani was horrified when the cake was cut and revealed the genuine Pinecrest Abbey Emerald necklace inside!

The Canine Crusaders sprang into action. General, ever the intrepid retired police dog, dashed through the halls, his comical raccoon-like appearance—the result of frosting-covered fur after a mishap involving the Suprise Cake—eliciting laughter from Gala attendees. His favorite four-letter word was "cake."

Aquila, with her keen eyesight and acute intelligence, made effective use of her Squawk Box, alerting the security team as the grifters tried to escape. She signaled General, the master of mischievous capers, to execute a daring plan. With stealth and agility, General, resembling a frosted raccoon more than a seasoned hero, darted toward the cake. In a furry flash, he snatched the concealed Pinecrest Abbey necklace hidden amidst the cake's layers.

Meanwhile, unaware of the hidden avian security guard, Giovanni, terrorized by dogs and now engaged in an unexpected chase, raced up the spiraling staircase. Little did he know that his fear awaited him at the top—Aquila perched in her beloved 35-foot Grove Giving Tree, a surprise encounter that left him frozen, stunned in disbelief.

As Giovanni reached the apex, General, still adorned in white cake frosting and now proudly clutching the stolen necklace, pressed a concealed button, transforming the staircase into a spiraling slide. With gravity as an uninvited escort, Giovanni descended—part exhilaration, part sheer panic—chased down the slide by none other than Aquila, the Bald eagle.

The room erupted into gasps and laughter as Giovanni, bewildered and now face-to-face with Aquila, echoed Mrs. O'Connell's iconic phrase, "Why is there a Bald eagle in the house?" The guests clapped at what they thought was an excellent Mystery Night performance of "The Grifters."

Mama Maria, the epitome of grace and poise, entered the scene, stunning the quartet with her presence. Their shock, however, soon turned into sheer horror as Mama Maria orchestrated an unexpected and uproarious revelation. Giovanni was horrified by her stern Mama Maria look when meeting his grandmother at the foot of the stairwell.

With the finesse of a seasoned maestro, she revealed her copy of the Pinecrest Abbey Emerald, perfectly adorning her neck, a sight that left the grifters speechless. Their carefully crafted plan unraveled before their eyes as Mama Maria unleashed a verbal thrashing, seamlessly weaving humor and humiliation.

With a swift flick of her wrist, she unveiled the ruse, exposing their attempted heist to the Gala attendees and turning their grand scheme into a jest among the gathered guests. The quartet caught off guard, found themselves at the receiving end of Mama Maria's playful reprimand.

As laughter echoed through the halls, Mama Maria, in her element, regaled the crowd with tales of the grifters' childhood antics, painting a vivid and comical picture of their past misadventures. The Gala transformed into a stage for amusement, where Mama Maria's unexpected presence and the grifters' folly became the highlight of the evening.

The quartet, once poised for triumph, now stood in the limelight of ridicule, outmaneuvered by Mama Maria and her unexpected yet brilliantly executed antics. The most humiliating and uproarious thrashing they could have ever imagined came not from the fury and feathered heroes, nor Detective Branagan, but from the indomitable force of Mama Maria, the matriarch of the North End!

Summary

"Pinecrest Abbey and the Artful Talon" unfolds within the rich landscape of Pinecrest Abbey, a haven nestled in New England, celebrating stewardship, conservation, and the vibrant partnership between humans and animals. At its core lies the awe-inspiring story of Aquila, a majestic Bald eagle, and her unique bond with the Canine Crusaders Security Team, exemplifying the triumph of nature's resurgence and humanity's responsibility.

The narrative traces Aquila's journey from a distressed eaglet to a guardian symbolizing vigilance and protection for the land. Her intelligence, aided by Winston Sterling's technology, and her playful escapades with the security team, paint a vibrant picture of coexistence and responsibility. Interwoven with Aquila's story is the saga of Sarah Kidd, echoing the Bald eagles' resilience from the brink of extinction to national emblem status. Sarah's tenacity mirrors the eagles' journey, blending past and present in Pinecrest Abbey's bustling halls.

The tale ventures into history, unveiling the legendary Pirate Queen Sarah Kidd's resilience amidst adversity. Her story, entwined with Captain Kidd's exploits and the enigmatic Bishop's Brig treasure, showcases her strength and reinvention in the face of trials. Amidst this, a quartet of grifters from Boston's Italian community plots a daring heist at the Grove Giving Gala. Isabella, Luca, Marco, and Giovanni, with their unique skills, converge to seize the prized Pinecrest Abbey Emerald, unaware of Mama Maria's unexpected intervention.

The Gala becomes a stage for revelation and amusement as Mama Maria foils the grifters' plan with wit and humor, turning their scheme into a comical jest. Their anticipated triumph dissolves into an evening of laughter and ridicule orchestrated by the formidable matriarch.

The narrative, an intricate tapestry woven with nature's resilience, historical echoes, and the vibrancy of the community, culminates in an unexpected turn of events that transforms the Gala into a tale of triumph—of humans, animals, and the indomitable spirit embodied by Pinecrest Abbey.

GOOD PUPPY STEP 10

Select a Trusted Dog Care Team

- Select a dependable friend or family member to act as your dog's godparent or guardian. But before making the decision, ensure they are both prepared and capable of handling this responsibility.
- Select a veterinarian, certified AKC dog trainer, groomer, and insurance company.

Name

Birthday

Breed

Special Memory

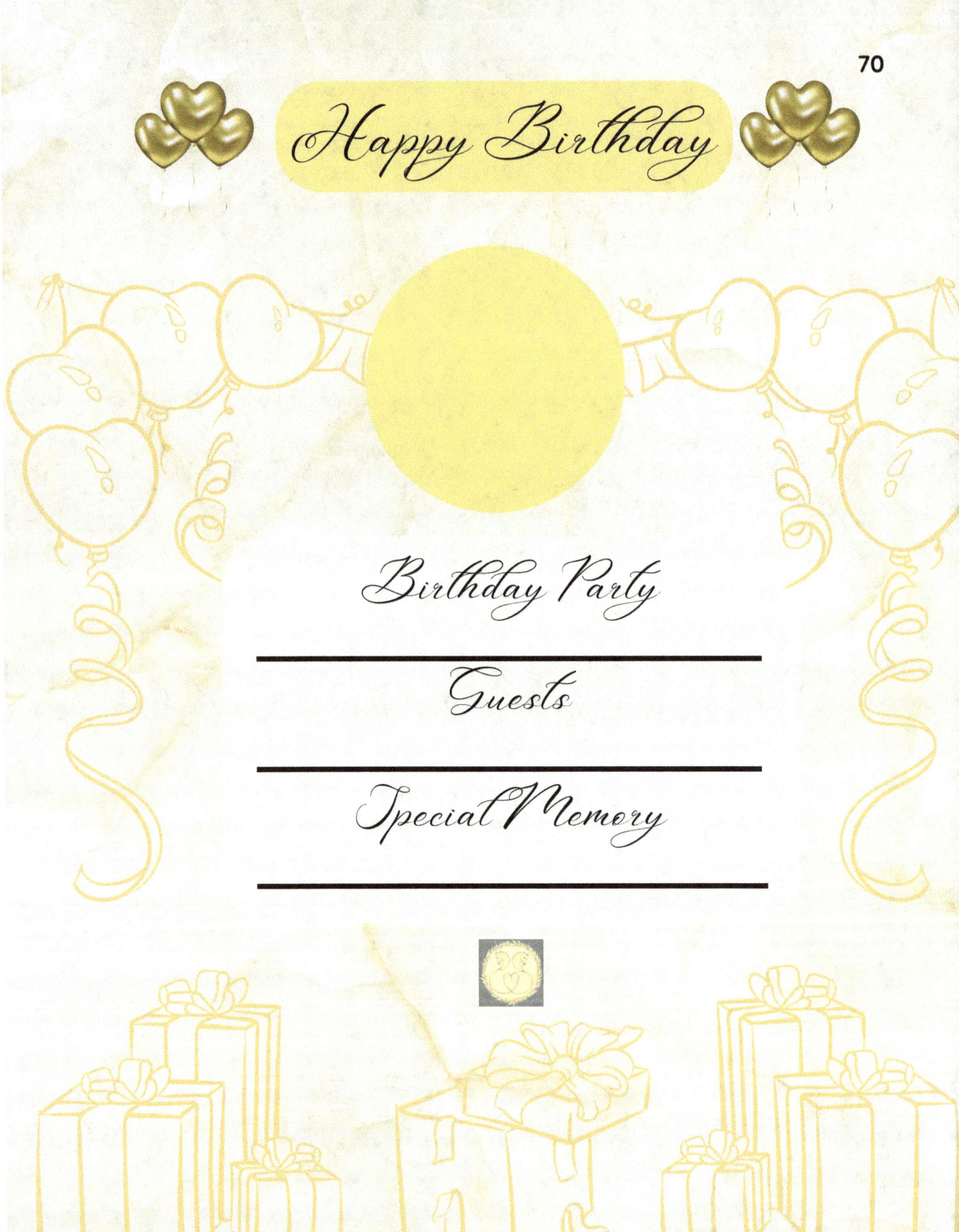

Happy Birthday
Birthday Party
Guests
Special Memory

First Christmas

____

Dog's Name

____

Special Memory

____

PUPPY-PROOF YOUR HOME
Checklist

- **Secure Hazardous Items:** Remove toxic foods, alcohol & cleaning products,
- **Electrical Cords:** Cover and remove electrical cords.
- **Small Objects:** Put away toys, jewelry, remote control, and cell phones.
- **Garbage Bins:** Store trash in a puppy-proof container.
- **Houseplants:** Ensure that any houseplants are non-toxic to dogs,
- **Furniture and Decorations:** Block off furniture to protect from dog's chewing.
- **Food and Kitchen Safety:**
  - Keep food out of reach on countertops.
  - Be cautious with hot stovetops and ovens.
- **Bathroom Safety:** Store toiletries and medications out of reach.
- Keep the toilet lid down to prevent your puppy from drinking toilet water.
- **Stairs:** Use baby gates to block off stairs until your puppy can safely navigate them.
- **Doors and Exits:** Ensure doors and gates leading outside are secure to prevent escape.
- **Cords and Blinds:**
- Secure window blind cords to prevent strangulation hazards.
- **Clothing and Shoes:** Keep out of reach.

PUPPY SAFETY RULES FOR KIDS
Do not blame the dog!

Good Puppy Step 5: Learn How to Understand Dog Behavior

Always Supervise: Never leave young children alone with a dog, regardless of how well you know the dog. Accidents can happen quickly.

Teach Respect: Teach your child to respect your dog's personal space and body. No pulling ears or tail, poking, prodding, or riding the dog.

No Startling or Sudden Movements: Instruct your child not to startle the dog or make sudden movements that could scare or provoke the dog.

Hands-Off Food and Toys: Teach your child not to approach a dog while eating, chewing a bone, or playing with a toy. dogs can be protective of these items. Stay out of the dog crate.

No Rough Play: Discourage rough play like wrestling or chasing the dog. Rough play can lead to misunderstandings and potential injuries.

Every dog is an individual. It is essential to understand your dog's temperament and behavior.

Be Calm and Gentle: *Encourage your child to approach the dog calmly and gently. Let the dog come to them if it feels comfortable.*

Recognize Signs of Stress: *Teach your child to recognize signs of stress in the dog, such as growling, showing teeth, or trying to escape. If the dog shows these signs, the child should back away slowly.*

No Sudden Hugs or Kisses: *dogs may not appreciate sudden hugs or kisses. Teach your child to approach the dog in a way that the dog is comfortable with.*

Teach Proper Petting: *Show your child how to pet the dog gently and avoid sensitive areas like head, ears and tail.*

Morning	Afternoon	Evening
6 AM Awake Good morning! Potty Break Take your dog out every 2 hours during the day. **6:30 AM** Zoomie Play Time Training Morning Walk **7 AM** <u>BREAKFAST</u> **7:30 AM** Potty Break **8 AM - 9 AM** Play Time **9 AM - 11 AM** Nap Time Puppies sleep a lot. Plan on daily nap times. **11 AM - 11:30 AM.** Potty Break	**11:30 AM - 12 PM** Zoomie Play Time Training Morning Walk **12 PM** <u>LUNCH</u> **12:30 PM** Potty Break **1 PM** Play Time **2 PM - 4 PM** Nap Time Puppies sleep a lot. Plan on quiet daily nap times **4 PM** Potty Break **2 PM - 4 PM** <u>PUPPY PARENT CLASS</u> Puppyparentbootcamp.com 10 Good Puppy Steps Class Online	**5 PM** Potty Break Take your dog out every 2 hours during the day. **5:30 PM** Zoomie Play Time Training Morning Walk **6 PM** <u>DINNER</u> **6:30 PM** Potty Break **7 PM** Play Time **8 PM** BEDTIME POTTY BREAK Take your dog out every 2 hours during the night if they are awake. Puppies will tell you if they need to go potty.

DAILY PUPPY CARE MENU
Well done, you got this!

Morning	Afternoon	Evening
7 AM BREAKFAST	12 PM LUNCH	6 PM DINNER

SPECIAL MOMENTS PHOTOS
Well done, you got this!

SPECIAL MOMENTS
Journal

Puppy Parenthood Do's & Don'ts

Puppy Parenthood is a rewarding, exciting, and challenging journey! It is essential to avoid making these common mistakes. By investing in your education, first prevent 3.1 million dogs (ASPCA) from entering animal shelters annually! Learn more about the 10 Good Puppy Steps class online at puppyparentbootcamp.com

- **Inadequate Education:** Pre-Puppy Parent training, education, and experience.
- Statistics show that 6.3 million animals enter shelters each year. (ASPCA)
- **Pets Are Not Gifts:** About 360,000 surrendered gift pets to animal shelters annually.
- **Discernment Disaster:** Discuss your decision to welcome a puppy into your home with Animal Services professionals.
- **Impulse Decision:** Getting a puppy without research, training, professional advice, or thought about what is best for the puppy. Puppies require time, care, money, and a lifetime commitment.
- **Quitting Parenthood:** Save a life, do not quit! Surrendering your puppy may cost them their life because of your mistake!
  - One-fourth – 1,575,000 dogs surrendered to animal shelters are pure breeds. (ASPCA)
  - Puppy 2.7 million cats and dogs annually are killed because shelters are full. (ASPCA)
- **No $ents:** Impulsively acquiring a puppy you cannot afford.
- **Manners Matter:** Do not blame the dog! Wait until the children are nine years old to get a puppy. Train your kids to treat and care for your puppy with respect and kindness.

Puppy Parenthood Do's & Don'ts

- **Socializing & Separation Storm:** Uneducated Puppy Parents make the common mistake of causing separation anxiety and socializing problems. Puppy Parents take an 8-week-old puppy away from their family before the puppy learns training and socializing skills at 3 - 4 months old. Dogs need their family to teach them how to establish hierarchy within the pack at 4 - 6 months.
  - Socialize politely with other dogs. Do not allow biting ears or tails and pinning other dogs on the ground.
- **Ignoring Health Care:** Not getting recommended shots. Avoid spaying or neutering before a puppy reaches one year old. Studies show it affects the maturing process. Research suggests breeds such as German Shepherds should not be neutered until they have reached 18 - 24 months to avoid health risks. Always discuss your dog's breed health decisions and requirements with a veterinarian.
- **Skipping Puppy Class:** Successful dog training typically involves a combination of factors, such as knowledge, patience, consistency, and environment, with an emphasis on positive reinforcement and understanding the individual needs and characteristics of your puppy.
- **Potty Pad Training:** Using potty pads teaches your puppy that your home is a bathroom.
- **Crate Training Incorrectly:** Crate training aims to provide a secure and comfortable space for your dog while ensuring their well-being and safety. Crates assist with potty training and help protect your home from chewing.

VACCINATIONS

There isn't a universal vaccination schedule. Instead, your veterinarian will personalize a vaccination plan for your dog, taking into account factors like breed, age, lifestyle, and where you live. This tailored schedule will suit your dog's specific requirements. Refer to AHAA vaccine guidelines.

Dog's Age	Recommended Vaccinations	Optional Vaccinations
8-11 Weeks	Distemper (Combination DA2PP)	
12-15 Weeks	Distemper (Combination DA2PP) Rabies	
16-19 Weeks	Distemper (Combination DA2PP) Rabies	
20-24 Weeks	Distemper (Combination DA2PP) Rabies	
24 + Weeks	Distemper (Combination DA2PP) Rabies	

PLACE YOUR PUPPY'S
PHOTO HERE

SPECIAL MOMENTS
Journal

SPECIAL MOMENTS
Journal

Weekly PLANNER

Weekly PLANNER

SUNDAY

MONDAY

TUESDAY

WEDNESDAY

THURSDAY

FRIDAY

SATURDAY

Weekly PLANNER

Weekly PLANNER

SUNDAY

MONDAY

TUESDAY

WEDNESDAY

THURSDAY

FRIDAY

SATURDAY

88
PLACE YOUR PUPPY'S
PHOTO HERE

SPECIAL MOMENTS
Journal

SPECIAL MOMENTS
Journal

Weekly PLANNER

SUNDAY

MONDAY

TUESDAY

WEDNESDAY

THURSDAY

FRIDAY

SATURDAY

Weekly PLANNER

SUNDAY

MONDAY

TUESDAY

WEDNESDAY

THURSDAY

FRIDAY

SATURDAY

Weekly PLANNER

SUNDAY

MONDAY

TUESDAY

WEDNESDAY

THURSDAY

FRIDAY

SATURDAY

Weekly PLANNER

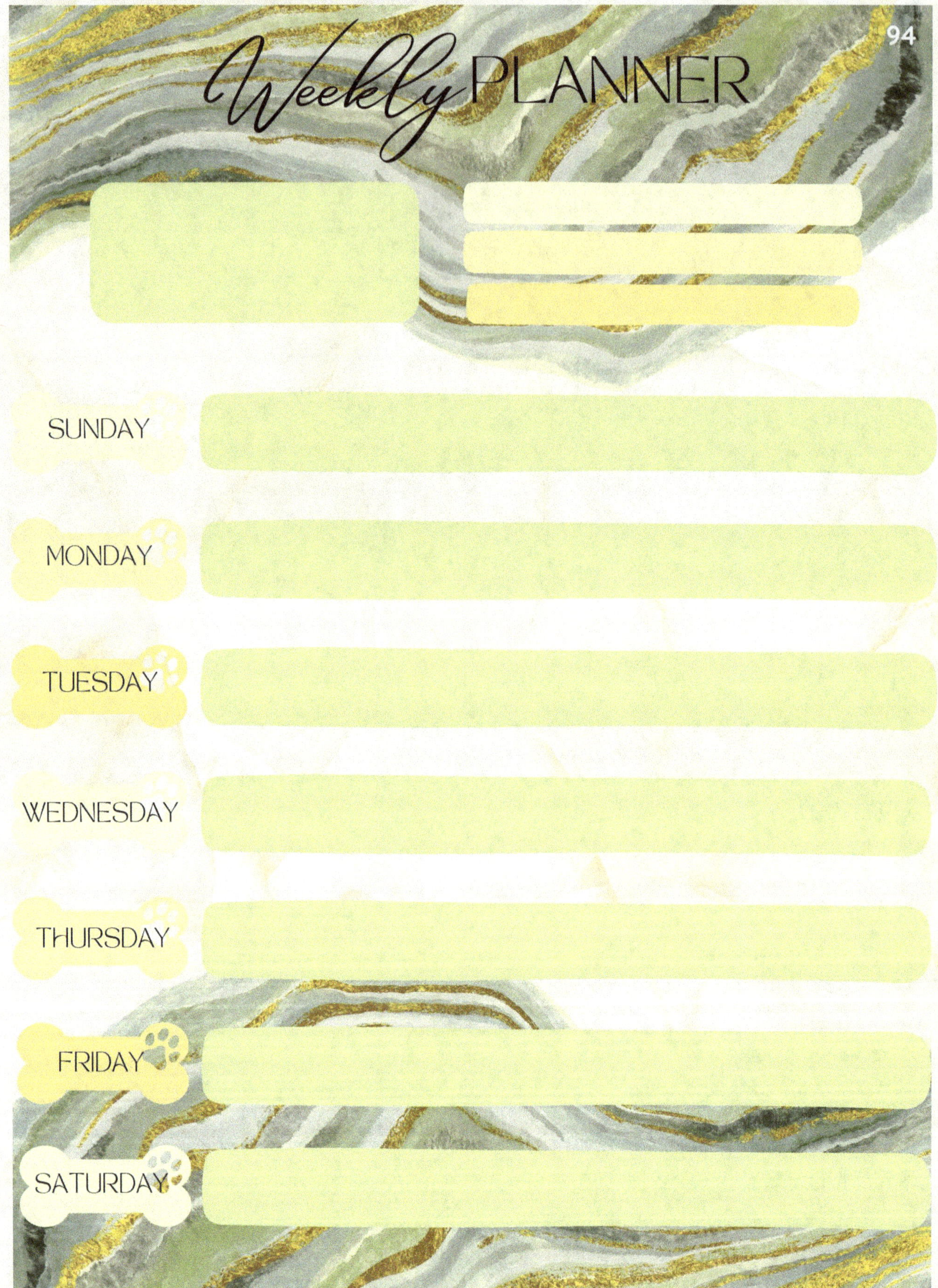

PLACE YOUR PUPPY'S
PHOTO HERE

SPECIAL MOMENTS
Journal

SPECIAL MOMENTS
Journal

Weekly PLANNER

SUNDAY

MONDAY

TUESDAY

WEDNESDAY

THURSDAY

FRIDAY

SATURDAY

SUNDAY

MONDAY

TUESDAY

WEDNESDAY

THURSDAY

FRIDAY

SATURDAY

Weekly PLANNER

SUNDAY

MONDAY

TUESDAY

WEDNESDAY

THURSDAY

FRIDAY

SATURDAY

Weekly PLANNER

SUNDAY

MONDAY

TUESDAY

WEDNESDAY

THURSDAY

FRIDAY

SATURDAY

PLACE YOUR PUPPY'S
PHOTO HERE

SPECIAL MOMENTS
Journal

SPECIAL MOMENTS
Journal

Weekly PLANNER

SUNDAY

MONDAY

TUESDAY

WEDNESDAY

THURSDAY

FRIDAY

SATURDAY

Weekly PLANNER

SUNDAY

MONDAY

TUESDAY

WEDNESDAY

THURSDAY

FRIDAY

SATURDAY

Weekly PLANNER

SUNDAY

MONDAY

TUESDAY

WEDNESDAY

THURSDAY

FRIDAY

SATURDAY

Weekly PLANNER
SUNDAY
MONDAY
TUESDAY
WEDNESDAY
THURSDAY
FRIDAY
SATURDAY

PLACE YOUR PUPPY'S
PHOTO HERE

SPECIAL MOMENTS
Journal

SPECIAL MOMENTS
Journal

Weekly PLANNER

SUNDAY

MONDAY

TUESDAY

WEDNESDAY

THURSDAY

FRIDAY

SATURDAY

Weekly PLANNER

Weekly PLANNER
SUNDAY
MONDAY
TUESDAY
WEDNESDAY
THURSDAY
FRIDAY
SATURDAY

Weekly PLANNER

SUNDAY

MONDAY

TUESDAY

WEDNESDAY

THURSDAY

FRIDAY

SATURDAY

PLACE YOUR PUPPY'S
PHOTO HERE

SPECIAL MOMENTS
Journal

SPECIAL MOMENTS
Journal

Weekly PLANNER

SUNDAY

MONDAY

TUESDAY

WEDNESDAY

THURSDAY

FRIDAY

SATURDAY

Weekly PLANNER

SUNDAY

MONDAY

TUESDAY

WEDNESDAY

THURSDAY

FRIDAY

SATURDAY

Weekly PLANNER

SUNDAY

MONDAY

TUESDAY

WEDNESDAY

THURSDAY

FRIDAY

SATURDAY

Weekly PLANNER
122
SUNDAY
MONDAY
TUESDAY
WEDNESDAY
THURSDAY
FRIDAY
SATURDAY

PLACE YOUR PUPPY'S
PHOTO HERE

SPECIAL MOMENTS
Journal

SPECIAL MOMENTS
Journal

Weekly PLANNER
SUNDAY
MONDAY
TUESDAY
WEDNESDAY
THURSDAY
FRIDAY
SATURDAY

Weekly PLANNER

SUNDAY

MONDAY

TUESDAY

WEDNESDAY

THURSDAY

FRIDAY

SATURDAY

Weekly PLANNER

SUNDAY

MONDAY

TUESDAY

WEDNESDAY

THURSDAY

FRIDAY

SATURDAY

Weekly PLANNER

SUNDAY

MONDAY

TUESDAY

WEDNESDAY

THURSDAY

FRIDAY

SATURDAY

PLACE YOUR PUPPY'S
PHOTO HERE

SPECIAL MOMENTS
Journal

SPECIAL MOMENTS
Journal

SUNDAY

MONDAY

TUESDAY

WEDNESDAY

THURSDAY

FRIDAY

SATURDAY

Weekly PLANNER

SUNDAY

MONDAY

TUESDAY

WEDNESDAY

THURSDAY

FRIDAY

SATURDAY

SUNDAY

MONDAY

TUESDAY

WEDNESDAY

THURSDAY

FRIDAY

SATURDAY

Weekly PLANNER
SUNDAY
MONDAY
TUESDAY
WEDNESDAY
THURSDAY
FRIDAY
SATURDAY

PLACE YOUR PUPPY'S
PHOTO HERE

SPECIAL MOMENTS
Journal

SPECIAL MOMENTS
Journal

Weekly PLANNER

SUNDAY

MONDAY

TUESDAY

WEDNESDAY

THURSDAY

FRIDAY

SATURDAY

SUNDAY

MONDAY

TUESDAY

WEDNESDAY

THURSDAY

FRIDAY

SATURDAY

Weekly PLANNER

SUNDAY

MONDAY

TUESDAY

WEDNESDAY

THURSDAY

FRIDAY

SATURDAY

Weekly PLANNER

SUNDAY

MONDAY

TUESDAY

WEDNESDAY

THURSDAY

FRIDAY

SATURDAY

Weekly PLANNER

SUNDAY

MONDAY

TUESDAY

WEDNESDAY

THURSDAY

FRIDAY

SATURDAY

PLACE YOUR PUPPY'S
PHOTO HERE

SPECIAL MOMENTS
Journal

SPECIAL MOMENTS
Journal

Weekly PLANNER

SUNDAY

MONDAY

TUESDAY

WEDNESDAY

THURSDAY

FRIDAY

SATURDAY

Weekly PLANNER

SUNDAY

MONDAY

TUESDAY

WEDNESDAY

THURSDAY

FRIDAY

SATURDAY

Weekly PLANNER
SUNDAY
MONDAY
TUESDAY
WEDNESDAY
THURSDAY
FRIDAY
SATURDAY

Weekly PLANNER

SUNDAY

MONDAY

TUESDAY

WEDNESDAY

THURSDAY

FRIDAY

SATURDAY

PLACE YOUR PUPPY'S
PHOTO HERE

SPECIAL MOMENTS
Journal

SPECIAL MOMENTS
Journal

Weekly PLANNER

SUNDAY

MONDAY

TUESDAY

WEDNESDAY

THURSDAY

FRIDAY

SATURDAY

Weekly PLANNER
SUNDAY
MONDAY
TUESDAY
WEDNESDAY
THURSDAY
FRIDAY
SATURDAY

Weekly PLANNER

SUNDAY

MONDAY

TUESDAY

WEDNESDAY

THURSDAY

FRIDAY

SATURDAY

158
Weekly PLANNER
SUNDAY
MONDAY
TUESDAY
WEDNESDAY
THURSDAY
FRIDAY
SATURDAY

PLACE YOUR PUPPY'S
PHOTO HERE

SPECIAL MOMENTS
Journal

SPECIAL MOMENTS
Journal

Weekly PLANNER
SUNDAY
MONDAY
TUESDAY
WEDNESDAY
THURSDAY
FRIDAY
SATURDAY

SUNDAY

MONDAY

TUESDAY

WEDNESDAY

THURSDAY

FRIDAY

SATURDAY

Weekly PLANNER
SUNDAY
MONDAY
TUESDAY
WEDNESDAY
THURSDAY
FRIDAY
SATURDAY

Weekly PLANNER

SUNDAY

MONDAY

TUESDAY

WEDNESDAY

THURSDAY

FRIDAY

SATURDAY

HOLIDAYS

DATE	HOLIDAY	DATE	PET HOLIDAY
JANUARY 1	NEW YEAR'S DAY	JANUARY	NATIONAL TRAIN YOUR DOG MONTH
THIRD MONDAY OF JANUARY	BIRTHDAY OF MARTIN LUTHER KING. JR.	JANUARY 14	NATIONAL DRESS UP YOUR PET DAY
		JANUARY 29	SEEING EYE GUIDE DOG ANNIVERSARY
		FEBRUARY	NATIONAL CAT HEALTH MONTH
		FEBRUARY	DOG TRAINING EDUCATION MONTH
		FEBRUARY	RESPONSIBLE PET OWNERS MONTH
		FEB.RUARY 20-27	NATIONAL JUSTICE FOR ANIMALS WEEK
THIRD MONDAY OF FEBRUARY	PRESIDENTS' DAY WASHINGTON'S BIRTHDAY	FEB.RUARY 20	NATIONAL LOVE YOUR PET DAY
		MARCH 23	NATIONAL PUPPY DAY

HOLIDAYS

DATE	HOLIDAY	DATE	PET HOLIDAY
		APRIL	PREVENTION OF CRUELTY TO ANIMALS MONTH
		APRIL 11	DOG THERAPY APPRECIATION DAY
		APRIL 30	NATIONAL ADOPT A SHELTER PET DAY
		MAY	NATIONAL PET MONTH
		MAY 8	NATIONAL ANIMAL DISASTER PREPAREDNESS DAY
		SECOND SATURDAY IN MAY	NATIONAL DOG MOM'S DAY
LAST MONDAY OF MAY	MEMORIAL DAY	MAY 20	NATIONAL RESCUE DOG DAY
		JUNE	NATIONAL FOSTER A PET MONTH
		JUNE	ADOPT-A-SHELTER-CAT MONTH
JUNE 19	JUNETEENTH	3RD WEEK IN JUNE	ANIMAL RIGHTS AWARENESS WEEK

HOLIDAYS

DATE	HOLIDAY	DATE	PET HOLIDAY
JULY 4	INDEPENDENCE DAY	JULY	NATIONAL LOST PET PREVENTION MONTH
FIRST MONDAY OF SEPTEMBER	LABOR DAY	AUGUST	CLEAR THE SHELTERS
		AUGUST	NATIONAL DOG MONTH
		SEPTEMBER	NATIONAL RESPONSIBLE DOG OWNERSHIP MONTH
SECOND MONDAY OF OCTOBER	COLUMBUS DAY	OCTOBER	ADOPT A SHELTER DOG MONTH
		OCTOBER 1	NATIONAL BLACK DOG DAY
NOVEMBER 11	VETERAN'S DAY	NOVEMBER	NATIONAL PET CANCER AWARENESS MONTH
FOURTH THURSDAY OF NOVEMBER	THANKSGIVING	NOVEMBER	ADOPT A SENIOR PET MONTH
		DECEMBER	NATIONAL CAT LOVERS' MONTH
		DECEMBER 2	NATIONAL MUTT DAY
DECEMBER 25	CHRISTMAS DAY	DECEMBER 13	NATIONAL HORSE DAY